CW00384010

FOR THE LOVE OF WILLIE

FOR THE LOVE OF WILLIE

AGNES OWENS

BLOOMSBURY

First published 1998

Copyright © 1998 by Agnes Owens

The moral right of the author has been asserted

Bloomsbury Publishing plc,
38 Soho Square, London WIV 5DF

A CIP catalogue record for this book
is available from the British Library

ISBN 0 7475 4011 X

10 9 8 7 6 5 4 3 2 1

Typeset by Hewer Text Ltd, Edinburgh
Printed in Great Britain by
St Edmundsbury Press, Suffolk

FOREWORD

Two patients sit on the veranda of a cottage hospital run by a local authority for females with mental problems, some of them long-term and incurable. Peggy, stoutly built, middle-aged, and with a hard set to her jaw, rises and stares down through the high railings at a bus shelter below.

'A man in that shelter resembles someone I once knew,' she tells her companion.

'Really?' says the companion, elderly and frail but known as the duchess because of her imperious manner. 'It beats me how you can remember anything.'

'I remember lots of things. That's why I'm writing a book.'

'A book? You never told me. What's it about?'

'About my life before they put me inside,' says Peggy. She adds wistfully, 'I had one, you know.'

'I can hardly imagine it,' says the older woman, whether referring to Peggy's earlier life or the book not being clear. 'Anyway,' she says snappishly, 'if you do manage to write a book who will read it? They're all simpletons here, including the staff.'

'I was hoping you might read it,' says Peggy, 'you being a highly educated woman with a superior knowledge of the frailties of the human heart.'

Her irony is lost on the duchess who says with a condescending smile, 'I might, if I've nothing else to read. But wouldn't it be better to get it published? Otherwise the whole thing could be a waste of time.'

'What does it matter?' asks Peggy. 'I've plenty of time to waste.'

ONE

'Wake up!' cried Peggy's mother, shaking her sleeping daughter in the bed recess of the kitchen where most of the house activity took place.

'Bloody well waken up, I said!' her mother cried louder as Peggy pulled the quilt over her head. From his bed on the other side of the wall her father shouted, 'What's all the racket about this hour in the morning?'

'She won't get up. She's supposed to start a paper round, but she can bloody well forget it if I've to go through this every time.'

Peggy jumped from the bed and stood shivering with her feet on the linoleum and her hands crossed over her chest. In place of a nightdress she wore her mother's black satin evening dress, a relic from the good old days before the war. It was too big for Peggy in every direction but she liked to stroke it under the covers. Her own tattered nightdress was now used for a duster. She

3

began raking the ashes in the fireplace, hoping to ignite a flame.

'Heat yourself over the gas ring,' said her mother. 'There's still some of last night's tea in the pot. Pour it out for yourself and make some toast. I'm going back to bed. I'm worn out getting up in the middle of the night to waken you, and don't touch the curtains or we'll be in trouble with the black-out people.'

'You mean the wardens,' said Peggy.

'Never mind what I mean. You get a move on or you'll be late. Personally I don't think it's worth the bother for the sake of a few bob —'

'I'm hurrying,' said Peggy.

She wriggled out of the evening dress and reached for her jumper. The sight of her daughter groping about in black school knickers and a dingy grey vest drove her mother to say, 'You might change your underwear once in a while.'

As Peggy stood over the gas ring waiting for the tea to heat up she lost all desire to leave the house and deliver papers in the cold and dark. Yesterday it had seemed a good idea when she spied a card in Willie Roper's shop window asking for a paper boy.

'Will I do instead?' she had asked him, excited by the smell of broken toffee in a tin on the counter. She could have nicked a piece if he had turned away.

'But you're a girl,' he had said.

4

'I can deliver papers as good as any boy.'

He had stroked his chin, looking her up and down. She had smiled back diffidently. It was easy to smile at Willie Roper with his reddish-brown curly hair and blue ingratiating eyes. He was slimly built, possibly in his late thirties and not much taller than herself.

'I suppose you could, but the papers have to be fetched from the railway station to the shop.'

'That's no bother.'

'It's only six shillings a week.'

'That's fine.'

She was overwhelmed by the sum of money. She would tell her mother it was four shillings and keep two.

'All right,' he said. 'Start tomorrow.'

She held out her hand to clinch the deal. The action seemed appropriate.

'Tell you what,' he said. 'Seeing as you're a girl I'll let you off with going to the station.'

He then handed her a bit of the toffee and she felt she was floating on air.

That had been yesterday. At this deathly hour she no longer felt like walking about in the black-out without meeting a soul. On the other hand Willie was now depending on her. At five to six she rushed along the dark empty street to the paper shop wearing her Sunday coat with a red pixie hat (one of a series she had knitted, huddled over the fire in the long winter evenings), also her mother's new suede shoes.

Two hours later she deposited the suede shoes under her parents' bed and returned to the kitchen where her mother stood over the stove stirring something in a pot.

'How did you get on?' she asked.

'It was OK,' said Peggy.

'Was Willie Roper pleased with you?'

'I think so. He was nice to me.'

'Oh yes, Willie's nice enough, but don't let him take advantage of you. He's a fly one, is Willie.'

'How do you mean?'

Her mother, not feeling able to discuss matters of a delicate nature with a daughter who appeared to move through life in a trance, said, 'Just keep your eye on him. No man's as nice as he looks.' She added with her eyes on Peggy's stocking soles, 'I hope you weren't wearing my good suede shoes.'

'Why should I? They're too big.'

'It's not the first time,' said her mother, frowning into the dried-egg mixture.

Her father entered the kitchen and said, 'Don't tell me it's *that* stuff again.'

'You're lucky to get anything,' said her mother. 'There's a war on.'

Peggy ate her breakfast with an air of contentment which had nothing to do with the food. Willie Roper had accompanied her on the paper round: 'To show you the ropes,' he had said with a grin. From his nods and smiles she thought she had managed well, though slightly discouraged by the way he blew his nose into a handkerchief then rubbed it hard as if to erase the snot. She forgave him when she remembered how her father picked his teeth with a matchstick and cut his toe nails on to the carpet. Her mother said all men were like that, with habits worse than dogs. There had also been a boy called Boris in the shop, who gave her a wink as they sorted out the papers before leaving to deliver them. He was tall, sallow-skinned, with jet-black hair; foreign-looking, she considered, but when she shyly asked Willie Roper if the boy was Italian, he had said with a contemptuous laugh, 'Irish.'

'I've to get four shillings,' Peggy told her mother.

'I thought it was five.'

'It's because I don't have to collect the papers from the station.'

'What did I tell you? Already he's taking advantage. You shouldn't stand for it.'

After a glance at Peggy's sullen face her mother added, 'Oh well, it's up to you. I'll save the four shillings until there's enough to buy you a pair of shoes when you get your next lot of clothing coupons.'

'Give her a shilling for herself,' said her father, wrapping a woollen scarf round his neck before leaving for the munitions factory. Her mother told him to mind his own business and get on his way, and after he left told Peggy, 'That was to save *him* giving you the shilling a week. He thinks I can't see through his little tricks.'

'Mother!' screamed Peggy. She sprang up in bed, looked round the ward, then sank back, dazed, against the pillow.

'What's wrong?' said the duchess, swinging her legs slowly over the side of her bed and sitting panting with a hand on her chest.

'I was dreaming.'

The old woman straightened her body and moved her head from side to side as if testing it for faults. She said, 'I dream a lot myself. It's like going to the cinema in a way.'

'Cover your legs,' said Peggy. 'They're like bones washed up by the tide.'

'The nurses say that for my age I've the best legs in the ward,' said the duchess, stretching them out to study them.

'At that rate when you're six feet under you'll have the best skeleton in the cemetery, if anyone cares to dig it up.'

Peggy jumped from her bed and reached out for the striped hospital robe saying, 'I'm off for a bath. I can't stand the smell of pee in this ward, especially first thing in the morning.'

The rest of the day was one of Peggy's bad ones. Days were mostly passed in static, stupefying boredom broken by exchanges of words, usually contentious, with the duchess. On her bad days she paced up and down the ward like a caged tiger.

'She reminds me of the woman in that film when she was about to be hung,' said a patient to the duchess. This raised no interest as she invariably said this when Peggy paced up and down.

'Never knew her,' snapped the old woman, immersed in a Mills and Boon romance.

She was more annoyed when Peggy stopped pacing to tell her, 'I wish someone would blow up this place and put us out of our misery, don't you?'

'Oh yes,' said the duchess without taking her eyes off the paperback and hoping Peggy would pass on. It was not to be. Peggy sat down beside her and asked if it was anywhere near the time for the sleeping pills, otherwise she might just slash her wrists.

The duchess looked at her own wrist (which had no watch on it) and said, 'It's early yet,' and added she didn't believe in taking sleeping pills since they were bound to be addictive.

'As if I care,' said Peggy. 'And is there any reason why I shouldn't be addicted?'

'None,' said the old woman, closing her book with a sigh. It was impossible to read with Peggy at her side. 'Especially when you're addicted already.'

'Who gives a shit?' said Peggy, throwing the book on to the floor. 'I'd rather be addicted to something than be a fraud like you.'

The old woman bent down and picked up the book.

'I don't know what you're talking about,' she said, searching for the place where she'd left off.

Peggy grew used to facing the cold and dark with the paper bag slung over her shoulder and had a distinct feeling of giving the public an essential service. Noisily she opened and closed gates and banged letter-boxes when shoving the papers through, hoping someone would come out and give a tip. All she received were angry words from the bedroom window of an irate customer, and a threepenny bit from an old woman who gave her a fright by waiting for her inside a porch. Her fingers were sometimes so cold that she heated them by putting them round her neck. When her mother told her to knit a pair of gloves Peggy said gloves were much harder to knit than pixie hats. Her mother then suggested cutting up a pair of old socks and making them into mitts, but Peggy said she wouldn't be seen dead with old socks on her hands. She also thought that, when she returned to the shop with her empty bag, the joy of warming her frozen fingers in front of Willie Roper's one-bar electric fire almost made the cold worthwhile.

'You'll get chilblains,' he would say, slipping her a chocolate-coated caramel and adding, 'Mum's the word.'

'I think Mr Roper's a smashing boss,' she confided to Boris one morning as they left the shop together.

'He's OK, I suppose.'

Detecting a note of disparagement in his voice she said, 'Don't you think he's smashing?'

'He's a boss, and you can't trust bosses.'

'He didn't say anything when you were late on Monday.'

'He knows better,' said Boris, as though he'd some sort of upper hand.

'How does he?' she said, then added inconsequentially, 'He says you're Irish.'

'I'm not,' he said. 'I'm the same as everybody else.'

'What does it matter?' said Peggy. 'So long as you're not a German.'

She offered him a caramel which had lain in her pocket since yesterday.

'Where did you get that?' he asked.

'Mr Roper gave me it.' The words were out before she remembered him saying, 'Mum's the word.'

'He did?' said Boris, surprised. 'Keep it. I've got something better.'

He brought out an oblong piece of tablet wrapped in newspaper.

'Did you get that with coupons?' she asked.

'I stole it when Roper wasn't looking,' he said, then broke it in two and handed her half. The next moment he leapt over a fence and through a garden to deliver a paper.

Peggy went in a different direction, thinking that he wouldn't be pleased to know she was given a caramel nearly every day.

In its second year the war was her parents' main topic of conversation, though each had a different interest in it. With her father it was the battle front. On coming home from work he repeated for their benefit all the reports they'd heard on the wireless and disregarded. With her mother it was the shortage of food and clothing.

'Isn't it ironic,' she said, 'that after all these years of being unemployed your father's got a good job in munitions and we can hardly buy a bloody thing?'

'Just thank your lucky stars they haven't called me up,' said her father.

'Yes,' said her mother doubtfully, thinking that a husband in the army earned more respect than a husband working in the munitions factory.

Peggy had no interest in the war. She had either her nose stuck in a book (as her mother described it) or was knitting her pixie hats with wool ripped out of old jerseys. An accumulation of pixie hats gave her a feeling of prosperity. The reality of the war only hit her when she was forced to accompany her mother into a cupboard under the stairs when the air-raid siren blew. They could have gone into the brick building across the road which was supposed to be a shelter, but some said it was so fragile a strong wind could blow it down.

'Why can't we stay in bed,' said Peggy. 'I've to get up early for my papers.'

'Do you want us killed because of your bloody papers?'

'I'd rather get killed than suffocate here,' said Peggy. But after five minutes in the cupboard Peggy was usually asleep under a pile of coats, while her mother remained wide-eyed and praying for the all-clear.

One morning the train carrying the papers didn't arrive in the station. The line had been derailed, not bombed as the paper boys were hoping, but a great cheer arose amongst them when Willie Roper told them to go home. On the spur of the moment, fearing she might not get paid for lost time, Peggy asked Willie if she could sweep out the shop. He frowned, scratched his head and said, 'All right, and while you're at it you can pack some shelves and put out the rubbish.'

The words rang like music in her ears, particularly when he added, 'If you do it right I'll give you an extra sixpence.'

'Sneaky bitch,' said Boris as he walked by her, but Peggy didn't care. She felt as if she'd been singled out for promotion.

TWO

Peggy and her parents lived in what would once have been described as a humble row of miners' cottages, but the gas mantle replaced the paraffin lamp, and some years later electric light replaced that, and with the installation of an inside toilet and bath they were much less humble and almost as good as modern council houses. If Peggy protested about having to bring a shovelful of coal from the outside bunker her mother would remind her how her grandfather had died along with twenty other men digging the stuff from below the ground when the old mine had been flooded years ago.

'Do you remember your da?' Peggy had asked.

'Of course I do. He was killed when I was no older than you. I remember him always black with the coal dust embedded under his skin even after soaking himself in the big tin bath in front of the fire.'

14

'I would love to have a bath in front of the fire instead of that freezing bathroom.'

'You wouldn't be so keen if you had to boil pots of water and run back and forward for twenty minutes to fill the bath, then run back and forward for another twenty to empty it.'

'I wouldn't care.' A thought struck Peggy. 'Did he sit in front of everyone naked?'

'He was covered up to his waist in water. Ma used to hold out a towel in front of him when he stepped out.'

Peggy giggled. 'You must have seen his bum.'

'Don't be so dirty. As if we cared about seeing our da's bum. It was hard times then. A lot harder than now, even with a war on. Anyway, bums were always on view in our family, getting leathered with a heavy belt. That's what you should get to knock some sense and respect for your elders into your head.'

'I'd run away if I got leathered.'

'Words are easy. Besides, your da is too soft with you. So am I for that matter.'

'Did you get leathered often?'

'Certainly. So did my two brothers and sister.' Peggy's mother smiled as if softened by a pleasant memory. 'I remember the time,' she said, 'when I accidently poured boiling water over his back before cooling it. He was reading his paper too.'

'Imagine reading a paper in the bath,' said Peggy.

'He always read the paper in the bath while either me or my sister scrubbed his back. When I poured the boiling water he nearly hit the roof like a scalded cat. Then he chased me round the room naked. I saw more than his bum that day. When he caught me he whacked me on the cheek so hard that I had a black eye for over a week. He was a hard man and I hated him most of the time, but I suppose he kept me in check.'

'Were you glad when he was drowned?'

'Good God, no! To think of my da's body floating in the oily water of the mine was more than we could bear. It took a long time to find him. All we remembered about him then were his good points. How he used to give us a halfpenny every week, which was fine in those days. In particular I remembered how I was the one who got his chop bone to lick when he was finished with it, and don't make a face, my lady, a chop bone then was better than a lollipop to us.'

To Peggy he sounded like a grandfather she had done well not to know, but she was impressed by the manner of his death. When she told Boris about it he wasn't.

'My great uncle got stuck up a chimney when he was cleaning out the soot. He choked to death and he was only sixteen.'

'That's strange,' said Peggy.

'What is?'

'If you think about it they both died because

16

of coal. When I look in the fire I'll remember my grandfather and your great uncle. I might see their faces in the flames.'

'Like ghosts?'

'Especially with the light off and the flames flickering round the room.'

'Don't get me all spooky,' said Boris. 'It's bad enough having to deliver to the house on top of the hill, and just when you're pushing the paper in the letter-box a tall man dressed in black opens the door and snatches the paper out your hand like a maniac.'

'I bet you it's only a butler.'

'They don't have butlers in bungalows.'

'How would you know if you've never been in one?'

'Anyway I hate the colour black,' said Boris. 'In all my life I'm never going to wear black.'

'Not even to funerals?'

'Not even.'

'What about your own funeral? Other people will be wearing black then. You can't stop them.'

'Shut up and don't talk about my funeral. You'll be dead long before me. Wait and see.'

He left for his paper route, hunched and hostile. Peggy hoped he wouldn't keep up his bad mood since she reckoned that she might have to marry him one day. He was the only boy she knew.

The duchess kept to her bed most of the time, except when forced out to the toilet. As she clung to Peggy's arm for support she murmured in a weak voice that she was sure she had suffered a stroke.

'Well, you don't look any different to me,' said Peggy.

'I was told that I fainted. How do you account for that?'

'I don't know about fainting. I remember you tried to attack me. Then you fell and banged your head on the locker. Is that what you call fainting?'

'That's not true,' said the duchess, stopping to pluck at her lip. 'You're saying that to make me feel bad. You know I have a weak heart. Even the nurse said that it was touch and go.'

'You can fool the nurse but you can't fool me,' said Peggy. 'I don't believe you. You'd say anything to get sympathy.'

She began pulling the old woman along.

'Don't walk so quick. You're making me breathless.'

'You're always breathless. There's nothing wrong with your heart or they wouldn't allow you up.'

'Oh leave me alone,' said the old woman, shaking herself free from Peggy in a spurt of energy. 'You're nothing but a cruel evil woman.'

'Evil?' said Peggy, with her hands on her hips. 'I like that. Who is it runs your errands and takes you to the lavatory and sits beside you when no one else will? Who does that, may I ask?'

With surprising spirit for someone who'd just had a stroke the duchess said, 'And who is it hides my walking-stick so that I can't get about, and who is it reads my mail when my back is turned?'

'What mail?' interrupted Peggy.

'And who was it stole my jotter?'

'Stole your jotter?' repeated Peggy, her face a study in bewilderment. 'Why, you gave it to me! Don't you remember the orderly told you she would bring in writing paper and envelopes which were more suitable for a person in your position, as you pointed out, instead of making do with a mouldy old jotter. You must remember that. Surely you're not in your dotage already?'

The duchess blinked in confusion. She placed her arm on the wall for support. A nurse came down the corridor.

'What's the problem, dear?' she asked.

The duchess was unable to think of an answer.

'It's OK,' said Peggy quickly. 'I'm taking her to the lav.'

She grabbed her companion's arm and they progressed slowly towards the toilet with the old woman staring backwards at the nurse as if there were things she had wanted to tell her.

'I don't know what's come over me recently,' she said. 'I can't seem to remember a thing.'

'Senility, that's what it is,' declared Peggy. 'It

comes to us all, but if you know what's good for you you'll try and buck up, for I don't want to go around with somebody that's in their dotage. You're bad enough the way things are. Anyway,' she added, 'I've got pages of my story done while you were snoring your head off.'

'What story?'

'My life story. Don't you remember me telling you about it?'

'Oh that.'

'Not that I expect you to appreciate it. Mills and Boon is more your line.' She squeezed the old woman's thin arm to make sure she was paying attention. 'Isn't it?'

'Not really,' said the duchess. They entered the toilet area which Peggy called the gas ovens and she hastened to add, 'I'm looking forward to reading your story, especially the bit about the man who was the father of your son.'

She broke off, partly because it was a sensitive subject but more because they were alone. Peggy, however, spoke quite blandly while shoving her into the toilet. 'I'm nowhere near there. You'll have to be patient.'

After carefully snibbing the door inside the duchess sat nodding her head with a mild form of paralysis.

An hour before the lights in the ward were dimmed Peggy looked over what she had written. Despite scorings out and possible misspellings she thought she had the start of a good story. It was a pity her only reader was a crazy old woman, but no one else in the ward seemed able to read, except herself of course, though she had never found anything worth reading in the hospital. She handed the jotter to the duchess who sat propped up on her pillow sucking a mint imperial from a secret store in her locker.

'Let me know what you think of it,' said Peggy, 'and don't sticky the pages with those mints you think I don't know about.'

The duchess suppressed a sigh. She had been looking forward to reading a tropical romance about a doctor and a nurse in a South Sea island hospital. It had as much in common with her surroundings as a cathedral has to a hen-house.

As the weeks passed the mornings gradually became less dark and cold, making the paper deliveries easier, but she missed the anonymity of darkness. People were inclined to get up early in the good weather and reprimand her for leaving their gate open, or not pushing the paper far enough through the letter-box, or (if she happened to be day-dreaming) delivering the wrong paper. When such mishaps resulted in a ticking off from Willie Roper it made her cheeks burn. But on the whole Peggy was happy in her job until the morning Boris told her that a dark-haired woman who occasionally hirpled through to the back shop on crutches was Willie Roper's wife.

'Wife?' said Peggy, drawing in her breath, as it had never occurred to her he had one. 'I thought she was his mother.'

'That's because she's got arthritis. My ma says he married her for the shop.'

'She owns it then?' said Peggy with a sense of doom.

'Yes, and their house above it, but she doesn't take anything to do with the shop. She leaves all that to him.'

'Thank goodness. I wouldn't like her to boss me around.'

'She's not all that bad,' said Boris. 'She gives me a sixpence if I get her a message.' He added meaningfully, 'No wonder.'

'What do you mean, no wonder?' said Peggy, annoyed and dismayed that no one had told her about Willie Roper's wife.

He hesitated then said, 'She always sends me for the same thing, a bottle of sherry. Sometimes she gives me a sip.'

Peggy was shocked. 'Gives you a sip of sherry?'

'I don't mind,' he said defiantly. 'She's opening the bottle anyway. I expect she's only wanting somebody to talk to.'

'Poor Mr Roper.'

'What's so poor about him? If she dies he'll get

the shop. My ma says she wouldn't be surprised if he puts poison in her sherry one day when she isn't looking.'

'I wouldn't believe that.'

'That's because you've got a crush on him,' jeered Boris.

'I have not,' said Peggy, flushing. 'But I don't think it's right that they're married.' She added with a furtive look at him, 'Especially if they sleep in the same bed.'

He shrugged. 'So what. I sleep with my big brother and I can't stand him.'

'It's not the same.'

'You mean,' he said, his eyes growing round, 'they might do dirty things?'

'You're a pig,' said Peggy, white at the idea of it. 'I don't want to talk to you any more.'

Sometimes she had fantasies about Willie Roper kissing her when a blast from a bomb had thrown them together on the floor of the shop, but nothing more. From furtive discussions with girls in the playground she knew vaguely what went on between men and women but couldn't relate it to Willie. She saw him more in the light of a saviour, or a tough guy with a heart of gold as depicted in the films.

'You started it,' said Boris angrily. 'I expect you're jealous.'

They parted cold and silent. Peggy decided that he wasn't the one to marry when he talked so dirty about Mr Roper. But that had happened a week past, and the subject was forgotten, especially when she hadn't seen Willie Roper's wife since. She had allowed herself one small image to make everything right in her head: Mrs Roper drinking alone from her bottle of sherry while Willie lay asleep in his bed in another room with an arm flung over his forehead, perhaps dreaming of a better life in which Peggy had a big part. Outside these preoccupations of the heart Peggy felt that in lots of ways things were looking up. For a start she had acquired a new pair of shoes.

'Don't think I haven't noticed that you're wearing mine,' said her mother, handing her a pair of clogs which were in fashion because they required no coupons. She could even afford to go to the pictures twice a week, and pay for a friend.

'Do you ever go to the pictures?' she asked Boris.

'Only gangster ones.'

She told him that she liked gangster pictures too and added, unable to stop herself, 'I think Mr Roper looks a bit like James Cagney, don't you?'

'All you ever think about is Willie Roper!' he groaned.

Once again they fell out over their employer, ruining Peggy's chances of asking him if he would accompany her to the next gangster film. She wanted this less out of affection for him than the status of being seen with a boy-friend.

When bombs fell on nearby cities Peggy told her mother that she would sleep permanently in the cupboard under the stairs because there was no way she could get up to deliver papers if every night she had to run back and forward to the air-raid shelter.

'I don't understand how you're so keen on that rubbishy job that you'd risk your life for it,' her mother grumbled, but without much emphasis. The air-raid shelter was something she now looked forward to. She'd wait up half the night for the siren to go, a flask of tea and sandwiches on the table, and her hair swept up into an elastic band which was the latest style. Peggy's father was now permanently on night shift. Part of his day was spent in the home guard which meant leaving the house in a khaki uniform and long boots he took an hour to polish.

'We have inspections just like the army,' he would say with an air of importance. If Peggy wasn't busy knitting her pixie hats she gave him a mock salute as he went out the door. Once he said, 'I hate leaving you two to the mercy of these German bastards.'

Her mother replied bravely, 'Don't worry about us, Robert. Just you do your duty and remember we are all in the hands of God.'

Peggy had stuck her tongue inside her cheek in

order not to laugh, though she supposed it was wise not to incur the wrath of God in the shape of a German bomb. Once inside the cramped space of the cupboard she felt safe because here was no room for the ghost she had once seen in the flames of the fire when sitting in front of it knitting a pixie hat. It was the face of an old man regarding her balefully. Realising this must be the face of her grandfather, she told it to go back to hell and prodded the coal with a poker.

'In the name of God, have you gone mad?' said her mother, slapping her cheek.

Peggy didn't answer. She knew she wouldn't be believed if she said what she'd seen. Besides, she had the feeling that she might be one of those people singled out to see what nobody else saw, somebody like Joan of Arc, for example. To talk about it would spoil everything.

THREE

For some peculiar reason all patients in the ward were served meals in bed, as if moribund or on the verge of it. The meals were predictable. Every weekday had its own speciality. Today being Tuesday it was liver. The duchess complained as if she was seeing liver for the first time.

'I can't eat this!' she said in a faint but peevish tone.

Peggy said, 'I don't care what I eat. It's all one to me.'

This was not true because if she didn't like what was on her plate she went to the veranda and threw it through the railings. Rats had been seen scampering in and out of the rhododendron bushes. The old woman cut her liver into small pieces then moved them round the plate with a fork as if playing a game of miniature chess.

'Back in your second childhood again?' asked Peggy.

The canteen woman passed back down with her empty trolley, paused at the duchess's bed and ordered her to stop messing about and get the food eaten.

'I'm not hungry. I've had a stroke, you see.'

'Liver's good for strokes,' said the canteen woman.

'Actually she's more used to a servant dishing her up venison,' said Peggy.

The canteen woman took this seriously.

'Oh she is, is she?' she said in a threatening tone.

The duchess dropped her knife on the plate and said timidly, 'If I could just have a cup of sweet milky tea —'

'You'll get that when you eat your liver! It's ridiculous wasting good food.'

The duchess shrank back on her pillow, blinked away tears in her eyes and put a small dice of liver in her mouth.

When the canteen woman left Peggy pushed her tray to the bottom of the bed, swung her legs on to the floor and said, 'You really ask for it, don't you?'

'Ask for what?'

'The way you draw attention to yourself all the time. It's a wonder they haven't done you in long ago. Give me that liver and I'll get rid of it.'

She grabbed the plate out of the old woman's shaking hands and pattered out to the veranda.

'I don't know what I'd do without you,' said the duchess when she returned.

'Always keep that thought in mind then,' said Peggy sternly.

When they were drinking tea afterwards the duchess said she thought what she'd read of Peggy's tale was most interesting and unusual. Peggy raised her eyebrows, staring hard at her companion.

'I mean it. It's really very interesting.'

'Don't overdo it,' said Peggy, looking pleased all the same. She added, 'It can't be any worse than those trashy books you read.'

'By the way,' said the duchess after a pause, 'have you seen the novel I was reading yesterday? I was going to lend it to one of the nurses.'

'I chucked it in the bin. It's the best place for it.'

'I suppose so,' said the duchess, turning away as the tears threatened to brim again.

'Don't worry. I'll try and have another chapter ready for you this evening,' said Peggy. 'Meantime I'm going out to the veranda to get a breath of air that doesn't have the smell of shit in it.'

One morning Willie Roper asked her to fetch a big ball of string from the back shop to tie up some old newspapers. She complied eagerly, always happy to oblige him and liking to study the shelves in there which were stacked with custard, tins of prunes, beans and all the food that didn't need coupons, besides ordinary stuff like sauce, salt, soap and soap powder. What most interested her was the

perfume and make-up and combs and kirby grips
on the shelf at the bottom. Lately she had bought a
lipstick called Pink Cyclamen which she only wore
outside the house. Boris said, 'God, your lips have
gone a funny colour,' but Willie Roper never gave
a sign he'd noticed. While bending down to pick
up a paper that had fallen on the floor, one of the
paper boys came in and put his hand up her skirt.
Peggy spun round, pale with affront.

'I'm telling Mr Roper on you.'

'Telling me what?' said Willie, appearing in the
doorway.

'He pushed me,' Peggy mumbled, her face
scarlet.

Willie looked at her intently then said to the
boy, 'You get through to the front. You've no
right being in here.'

Then he asked Peggy if she was sure that was
all he did. Peggy thought she was going to faint
with embarrassment, especially when he put his
arm round her shoulder and said, 'Maybe he did
something else?'

She shook her head and stared down at the
floor, hiccuping with nerves.

'Look,' said Willie, his mouth close to her ear,
'don't worry about it. It's not your fault you're
turning out to be a right pretty one.'

For a second she thought he was going to
do the same as the paper boy but when she
finally managed to look round at him his face

was all concern. At that moment she thought she'd never loved him so much. This made the blow harder when next morning he told her Mrs Haddow had cancelled her papers because Peggy had left a garden gate open, and as a result her dog disappeared for three hours and returned with an ear chewed off by another dog.

'But I did close the gate! Perhaps it was the postman.'

'It's no good blaming the postman. The dog had disappeared before he arrived. You've lost me a customer.'

Peggy was appalled by the cold and stern look on his face. She was about to walk out rather than wait for the sack when he said less severely, 'Try and be more careful about closing gates in future. The woman's a complaining old bag but that's beside the point.'

Peggy, close to tears, nodded and began folding up her papers. Not even a sympathetic nudge from Boris who stood beside her folding his own cheered her up. Outside the shop she told him, 'I know I closed that gate. Why did he have to believe Haddow and not me?'

'I told you bosses were like that,' said Boris. 'One minute all sugar the next minute all shite. He took sixpence off my wage last week when I slept in. As if it made any difference. I still had to deliver the same amount of papers. I tell you he's

as mean as get out. You should hear what my ma
has to say about him –'

'I don't want to talk about it any more,' said
Peggy, her anger against her boss evaporating when
she remembered the shivery sensation in her spine
as he put his arm round her shoulder. 'Anyway
there's no point in him being a boss if he can't
tell people off.'

'Oh yeah?' said Boris scornfully. 'He's a pig. If
it wasn't for Mrs Roper he would have got rid
of me long ago. Do you know I've to sneak up
the back stairs when he isn't looking to give her
the sherry? The less he knows the better, she told
me, and that's his wife.'

'I thought she'd the final say in everything.'

'Not about the sherry. He thinks it's a disgrace
for women to drink.'

'And so it is.'

'If you were in pain with arthritis maybe you'd
want to drink. She says it's the only time she
feels well.'

Peggy gave an exaggerated shudder. 'I'd hate
to have to go for sherry.'

'That's because you're a snob. By the way, she
once asked me about you.'

'Asked about me?' said Peggy, scandalised. 'What
did she say?'

'She asked me why you don't collect the papers
at the station the same as everybody else.'

'What did you say?'

'I said maybe it was because you were a girl, but I wasn't sure.'

'And then what?'

'She just went "Mmm" –' He broke off. 'Look, I'm away before the customers start complaining about me next. Not that I'm bothering.'

Peggy watched him go, feeling uneasy at the thought of Mrs Roper asking about her.

In the same week an incendiary bomb fell near a bus stop where her father was waiting after leaving his work. He died instantly with a piece of shrapnel in his head and that finished Peggy's paper job. At the funeral service her mother had sobbed into a handkerchief at the loss of a husband whom previously she had considered no great asset, while Peggy sobbed at being removed from Willie Roper's newsagent's.

Her mother had said, 'I won't have you leaving me alone in this house while you go skedaddling all over the place in the early hours of the morning. You could get killed the same as your dad and then where would I be?'

Peggy felt that if she couldn't see Willie Roper again she would like to get killed. Later that evening her mother came into her bedroom and told her to cheer up. She would get over her father's death in time.

The duchess slept badly that night, tossing and turning and calling out the names of people Peggy had never heard her mention before. Finally she sat up and asked Peggy to get her a bedpan.

'Get it yourself,' said Peggy, punching her pillow in temper.

'I can't. If I move I'll wet the bed.'

'Wet it then and give us all peace.'

'The nurse will hit me. You know what they're like.'

Peggy stabbed her forefinger into the bell above her head.

'They're going to hit you anyway when they find out you've wakened half the ward.'

Further along the ward a woman had begun to shriek and another one was banging her head on her locker. A nurse came whirling in to ask what the racket was about.

'It's her,' said Peggy, pointing to the next bed. 'She wants a bedpan.'

'A bedpan?' said the nurse, raising her thinly pencilled eyebrows at the duchess who sat cowering. 'Surely she's not so incapacitated that she can't walk to the toilet?'

'I think I'm going to wet the bed any minute,' the old woman quavered.

'Why didn't you go earlier?' said the nurse, jabbing her on the chest.

'It came on me all of a sudden.'

'And let's face it,' said Peggy, 'it's not easy to go for a piss in this place. You're liable to get beaten up for walking along the corridor.'

'You mind your own business,' said the nurse, staring down the ward to where patients were either sitting up in bed or walking in circles weeping and wringing their hands. She took off towards them at a run and after a good deal of persuasion and threats managed to get them back to their beds. She returned to the duchess flushed and dishevelled.

'Listen,' she said. 'I'll get you a bedpan this time but I warn you, try it with me again and I'll give you such a smack on the bottom you won't be able to sit down on anything, let alone a bedpan.'

When she left Peggy turned to her companion and said, 'I like the way you stuck out for that bedpan. For once you got the better of her.'

The duchess said nothing but stared sorrowfully at the ceiling while a warm stream of urine spread over her thighs and down her legs.

'You're surely not going out?' Peggy's mother called from her bedroom as Peggy passed the door.

'I need some fresh air. My head's stuffed up with being indoors all the time.'

'You know I can't bear being left on my own,' said her mother in the plaintive tone she'd adopted since the funeral. Peggy looked at her mother flicking through the pages of a woman's magazine with a bored expression on her face.

She said, 'If I was at school you'd have to be on your own.'

'But you've only a few weeks to go. They won't be expecting you back now under the circumstances.'

'I'm going out,' said Peggy defiantly.

'All right then,' said her mother. 'We'll both go out and visit your father's grave. It will be nice to look at the marble headstone again.'

'I don't count that as being nice,' said Peggy, who could not connect a marble stone with the last sight of her father polishing his boots before leaving for the home guard. In the cemetery her mother had looked at the inscription *Forever in our Hearts* and said, 'So tasteful!'

'Is it?' Peggy had said, looking with detestation along the row of similar inscriptions on similar stones.

'All right, go out,' her mother now said with a sigh. She was tiring of her role as a grieving widow. Resentment had become what she mainly felt at a husband's death which had not been exactly in his line of duty.

Once outside Peggy approached Roper's shop with a sinking heart. What if he had somebody else in her place? She went round to the back of the shop and to give herself time to think sat at the bottom of the stairs leading up to Willie Roper's house. Suddenly a voice called from the top of the stairs saying, 'Will you come up a minute?'

Peggy looked upwards and was shaken to see Willie Roper's wife on the landing.

'Come on,' shouted the woman. 'I won't eat you.'

Peggy climbed slowly to confront the woman who from close up was quite attractive. Dark eyes contrasted well with a pale complexion and black curling hair gave her the appearance of a gypsy.

'Would you mind going a message for me?' she asked.

Peggy wanted to refuse but she couldn't find the words. Mrs Roper must have taken her silence as agreement. She said, 'Come in.'

The room was surprisingly clean and cheerful for a woman who couldn't move about easily. A bright fire burned in the grate and there was a vase of flowers on the table. She took a purse from a drawer and handed Peggy silver saying, 'Are you the girl who used to deliver the papers?'

'Yes,' said Peggy hoarsely.

'I don't see you coming any more. Did he give you the sack?'

'If you mean Mr Roper, no. My da got killed with a bomb and I couldn't leave my ma alone in the house.'

Mrs Roper tutted and shook her head. 'What a tragic thing to happen. But it's always them that's needed that gets snatched off and them that isn't that's left to rot.'

She showed Peggy her hands with the knuckles twisted and enlarged.

'Arthritis,' she said.

Peggy gave her a thin smile of sympathy, wishing she was far away from this woman with the knowledgeable eyes. She looked at the silver in her hand and said, 'What is it you want me to get?'

'A bottle of sherry,' said Mrs Roper. 'If you don't mind.'

FOUR

'My, my, you're a stranger,' said Willie Roper when she walked into the shop and bought a *Schoolgirl Weekly* with the sixpence his wife had given her. 'I thought I would have seen you before this.'

'It was my da,' she began. 'He died and I −'

'I know,' he said, becoming serious. 'It's been a rotten time for you and your ma. If there's anything I can do, let me know.'

She took a deep breath and asked him if she could have her job back. He frowned and scratched his head.

'It so happens I had to get someone else when you didn't come. I kept the job open for a week but when Boris left to join the army cadets I was in the soup. So you see −'

'It's all right,' she said, turning away as a customer came up to the counter.

'Hey, wait a minute,' he called. 'When do you leave school?'

'In two months.'

When he told her to come back then and he would give her a part-time job behind the counter she couldn't believe her luck.

'You're not going,' said her mother.

'Why not?'

'It's only common types who work in shops. Your father and I always wanted you to work in an office where you meet a better class of people.'

'I don't want to work in an office,' said Peggy. 'Only snobs work there. I've always wanted to work in a shop and it's my life, not yours.'

Her mother regarded her with a look of pity and said, 'Normally I wouldn't care where you worked, but I do draw the line at working for Willie Roper. Maybe you don't know this but he gets the name of being fond of young girls, and I don't mean in a nice way. I thought it was bad enough when you were going with his papers but I let it slide because I knew it wouldn't last for ever, and now here you are going to work in his shop. Well I –'

'I don't care what you say,' said Peggy. 'Willie Roper is a gentleman and I know him better than you. I'm going to serve in his shop and you can't stop me.'

The duchess was moving around better than she'd ever done before. She'd discarded her walking-stick and didn't ask for help when going to the toilet. Her manner had also become studiously polite to everyone, particularly the patients. She went round them asking how they were keeping, even though they backed away from her in alarm. Peggy viewed this change with suspicion.

'Are you all right?' she called out, seeing her companion nimbly approach the swing doors, presumably to go to the toilet.

'Of course I am all right. Why shouldn't I be?'

'I don't know. It's just that you seem to have got a new lease of life and I'm damned if I know why.'

'I feel much better than formerly,' declared the duchess with a cheerful laugh.

'I'd watch out if I was you. They say a light bulb flashes its brightest before it goes out.'

'I'm not interested in light bulbs,' said the old woman, nipping through the door.

Peggy got hold of the nurse who was dishing out the evening dose of sleeping pills.

'Listen,' she said, 'you'd better watch out for the duchess. She's gone out the door as fast as a two year old. I wouldn't be surprised if she's on the verge of a breakdown and slashes somebody with a dinner knife.'

The nurse gave an inane laugh somewhat similar to some of the patients'.

'Don't be silly. She hasn't got the stamina.'

'Well, she had the stamina to stab her husband to death,' said Peggy. 'At least that's what she told me.'

'She doesn't know what she's saying,' said the nurse. 'She's crazy.'

'I know that,' said Peggy. 'And now she's crazier than ever. Aren't you going to do something?'

The nurse tutted and walked down the ward shaking her head. Then the duchess returned to the ward and asked Peggy what month it was.

'March, I think.'

'Good, I'll be getting out soon. My husband's coming to take me away at the beginning of April. It's all been a ghastly mistake me being in here, you know.'

'I thought your husband was dead,' said Peggy.

The duchess stared at her, exasperated. 'I don't know where you got your information, unless it's from the staff who are all pathological liars, but I can assure you my husband is alive and well and is coming for me soon and I'll have to have all my wits about me when I walk down those high stone stairs. That's why I'm not taking any sleeping pills. However I don't want to discuss it at present.' She gave Peggy a bright smile. 'So how is your writing coming on, dear?'

'Not bad,' said Peggy.

'That's the spirit. Keep writing and get it all out of your system, and don't forget to let the world know what is going on in here, how they keep us doped up most of the time so we won't complain. You tell them –'

'That reminds me,' said Peggy. 'Have you any writing paper to spare? My jotter's almost used up.'

The duchess's face became hostile. 'Excuse me,' she said. 'I'll have to go and ask the nurse to give me something for a sore head. An aspirin will do.'

Willie Roper kept his word and Peggy got the part-time job of stacking shelves, sweeping the floor, folding papers and making tea for them both in the afternoon. They did not take it together, but Peggy was glad. It saved her the embarrassment of eating in front of him and making conversation. She was still in love with him, she supposed, but not as much as the day he'd put his arm round her shoulder, which likely hadn't meant a thing. He'd only been trying to comfort her. Some men were like that, 'the fatherly type' they were called, so now she found it easy to face Mrs Roper on Friday night when fetching her sherry. She had inherited Boris's job.

One morning a box of loose custard was delivered to the shop and Peggy was asked to stay through lunchtime to help make it up into small bags, for which she would be paid an extra two shillings. This turned out to be a messy business. Her blue angora jumper, actually her mother's, became covered with the stuff. She tried to wipe it away but it became all the more engrained. Noticing this, Willie took a brush from a drawer and began brushing her down, first at the back, then at the front, going very carefully over her chest. Peggy's face was burning. She hoped he didn't notice.

'That's better,' he said, standing back to survey her. Peggy closed her eyes and tried to think of buckets of ice in order to cool down. The next thing his arms were round her waist. She pulled herself away.

'I'm sorry,' he said, immediately contrite.

'That's all right,' she said, amazed that her voice sounded so composed when inwardly she was shaking. The following morning he asked her to stay on again at lunchtime. She wondered why. All the custard had been packed. But it was no surprise when he came into the back shop and kissed her on the cheek, saying he was mad about her and couldn't help himself and would she forgive him?

'Of course,' she said, smiling at him tenderly then going on to say that she'd always been mad about him from the first day she'd delivered the papers. After that there was no need for them to say any more.

A week later he bought her a black handbag and promised her a ring, nothing too flamboyant, he said. Just a plain silver one to plight their troth. She thought the words 'plight their troth' were the most exquisite she'd ever heard, though he explained in the next breath she'd have to wait until they could slip away to a jeweller's out of town so that she could get the right size. She said she didn't mind waiting.

'What's come over you these days? You look as if you're sleep-walking half the time,' said her mother, putting on her coat. She was going out with a friend to the pub as she usually did on Friday after coming home from the munitions factory.

'I'm tired, that's all,' said Peggy.

'I don't know why. You only work half a day and do damn all the other half as far as I can see. I hope you manage to wash these dishes before I get back.'

Peggy nodded, her eyes fixed somewhere in the distance.

'Another thing I've noticed,' said her mother. 'You're never outside the house except to go to that job of yours. Why don't you join something like the badminton club? It would give you an interest instead of sitting in here moping. It's not natural.'

'I thought you didn't like me going out.'

'That was just after your father died. You could hardly expect me to be on my own then. But it's different now. You should be out enjoying yourself.'

That's because you're out all the time and feeling

guilty, Peggy thought, but didn't much care. Her mother could do what she liked as long as she kept her nose out of Peggy's affairs. But sometimes her mother's words struck home. Perhaps it wasn't natural staying in so much and listening to the wireless. She'd stopped knitting pixie hats. But mostly her mind was occupied by Willie Roper and what they did on the floor of the back shop during the lunch break.

When he came to the door one evening she nearly fell down with shock and pleasure.

'Willie,' she breathed. 'What are you doing here?'

'Is your ma in?'

'No.'

'That's what I was hoping.'

As she showed him into the living-room it struck her the place looked a mess. Clothes lay over chairs, an ironing-board stood in the middle of the floor; for the first time she noticed the dust on the sideboard.

He planked himself down on an easy chair and told her to come and sit on his knee. Shyly she complied, thinking how handsome he looked in his grey pin-stripe suit and more like James Cagney than ever. She asked if there was anything wrong.

'No, my love,' he said. 'I just happened to be passing on my way to a boring committee meeting at the bowling club and thought I might as well look in.'

He took a flat-sided bottle from his pocket and offered it to her.

'What is it?' she asked.

'Gin. It's good for you in small doses.'

'I don't know,' she said, remembering with wonder how Willie didn't like his wife drinking.

'A spot won't do you any harm.'

'All right,' she said, thinking, why not? This visit was as good as anything she could wish for. She took a sip and shuddered. He laughed and whispered in her ear, 'How about going into the bedroom?'

'All right,' she whispered, the bottom of her spine beginning to tingle.

Twenty minutes later they were back in the living-room. Willie looked at his watch and said he would have to fly.

'Can I come with you?' she asked on an impulse.

'To a committee meeting?' he said, aghast.

'I could wait outside until it was over. Then we could go somewhere and –' She broke off when she saw the angry look on his face.

'If people saw us together outside the shop they'd put two and two together and then what do you think would happen?'

She shook her head shamefacedly.

'I could go to jail. You must know that you're

considered a minor if you're under eighteen, though God knows you could pass for eighteen any day.' Then he added, 'Don't look so despondent, darling. Do you still love me?'

'You know I do,' she said. 'I didn't realise what I was asking. Do you still love me?'

'Of course I do, you silly girl,' he said. He tweaked her nose and was gone.

FIVE

Mrs Roper asked Peggy if she was in the habit of reading books.

'Sometimes,' she replied, dreading what was coming next and wanting to get away as quickly as possible. She hadn't minded fetching the sherry when it was just a matter of purchasing it and handing it over but the woman now persisted in asking her in.

'I've got this terrific novel called *The Plague* by a man called Camus,' she said. 'You should read it. I'm sure you'd like it. A good book helps you to understand yourself as well as others.'

Before Peggy could say anything Mrs Roper had thrust the book into her hand.

'I know everyone hasn't got the same taste when it comes to books but –'

'Thanks,' said Peggy, not wanting to prolong the subject and finding it difficult to look her in the eye. She'd once asked Willie why he didn't buy sherry for his wife. He had said that he didn't want to encourage her to drink, which seemed strange since he drank himself.

'Besides,' he'd added, 'she likes seeing you. It breaks her day.'

From Peggy's point of view that made it all the worse.

'Though perhaps you've better things to do with your time than read a book,' said Mrs Roper, unscrewing the bottle top.

Peggy turned red, sensing some kind of implication.

'Not really.'

'I thought you might have a boy-friend?'

'No,' said Peggy, becoming agitated.

'I'm surprised. You're a pretty girl. Still, I suppose you're better not to rush into things. I did, and look at me.'

'You mean you got married?'

'Don't take me seriously,' Mrs Roper had said. 'My husband's a good enough man. He doesn't like to see me drinking, and who can blame him? But you see it's the pain. I always have this terrible pain.' Then she broke off. 'But I shouldn't be talking like this. I'm sure you won't repeat anything I say.'

'Oh no,' said Peggy, and said she would have to leave, her mother would worry if she stayed out too long.

'Of course she will,' said Mrs Roper, 'and she's quite right. Young girls are always so vulnerable.'

Peggy wondered if there was a hidden meaning in her words. Was it possible she knew what was going on between her and Willie? Her fears were dispelled when Mrs Roper called over the railings that she hoped to see her the following Friday.

As weeks turned to months she grew more and more dissatisfied with the way they had to be furtive about everything, even the single glance that might betray them to a customer. Yet she knew it had to be this way for her mother would kill her if she found out. But despite her mother's poor opinion of Willie Roper she remained strangely unsuspicious. Once, in connection with Peggy's stopping on at lunchtime, she said she hoped Peggy was being paid for the extra hour and if so why didn't she hand over the money? Peggy's answer was to leave the room suddenly as if she had something urgent to do. After that the matter seemed to be forgotten.

One day, being in a particularly anxious mood, she asked Willie if he still slept with his wife.

'Of course not. What kind of a person do you think I am?'

'Then why don't you put in for a divorce? By the time I've turned eighteen we can get married.'

He looked at her, frowning. 'How do you know you'll still love me when you're eighteen?'

'I'll always love you.'

'That's easy to say now but you might not say it then.'

She didn't argue about this as she could see he was becoming annoyed. The next time the subject of divorce cropped up he said that there was no way he could abandon his wife when she was in such poor health.

'Besides,' he added, 'the shop is hers and without it I'd have nothing.'

When Peggy said she didn't care as long as they were together as man and wife he said she must give him time to think about it. In the meantime they would just have to carry on the way they were.

A day came when they were bold enough to take a journey into the country, travelling in separate buses then meeting on the outskirts of a field where there was not a soul in sight except some distant cows. Peggy thought it was wonderful to lie on the grass like any other courting couple. They ate Spam sandwiches she had made up at home and drank beer out of bottles. She disliked the beer's bitter taste and would have preferred lemonade, but drank it anyway. It made her head spin. It also made Willie belch a good deal, which he did loudly and without excusing himself. She disliked that. When he tried to push her down on the grass she told him to leave her alone as she was feeling sick, then she got up and walked aimlessly round the field. He was sitting on the same spot when she returned, his face red and angry.

'What's wrong with you?' he said.

'I told you beer made me sick.'

'At that rate we'd better go home.'

Before they separated to go back on different buses they made it up again. Yet at the same time she felt as dismal as though they hadn't. Over and above that she had a splitting sore head. She put this down to the fact that her period was late.

For two days the duchess had either been sitting in a trance or dozing off except when hauled to the toilet by Peggy, who got a certain amount of satisfaction from seeing her old friend dependent on her. Now in the late afternoon of a cold spring day she sat on the veranda with Peggy who stood with her back against the railings saying, 'It serves you right for refusing your pills. You should know by this time they'd only make you swallow double. Whatever made you do it?'

'Mind your own business,' said the old woman, 'and take me inside.'

'Take yourself inside,' said Peggy. She turned and looked through the railings, then became excited. 'Look, he's back again. I knew he'd come back.'

'Who's back?'

'The man that was there before.'

'Oh,' said the duchess. 'If you'll just give me your arm I'll manage once I get inside. I don't know why I came out in the first place.'

Peggy wasn't listening. She was shouting through

the railings, 'Come on up. We're in ward A, first on the left.'

'I'm sure I don't want any undesirables visiting me,' said the duchess.

Peggy became more excited. 'He's on his feet and looking up here. I do believe –' Then she sagged and said, 'Damnation and blast. He's walking away.'

The duchess said, 'That's because you frightened him off. One look at you and anybody would be frightened.'

'If anyone frightened him off it would be you,' said Peggy.

They both went silent after that. A drizzle of rain began to fall.

'Funny thing,' said Peggy. 'I usually feel better when it rains.'

'Well, I don't,' said the duchess, pulling the shawl up over her chin. 'I'm likely to catch my death out here.'

'Go in then and give us peace.'

'If I do they'll pick on me. They're always picking on me.'

'They pick on everybody.'

'They pick on me the worst. God, I wish I was dead.'

'You will be one day.'

'And you'll be glad, I suppose.'

'I won't know until it happens.'

'And I thought you were my friend too,' said

the old woman, wiping her watering eyes on a corner of the rough material.

Peggy gave her an odious look. 'How can I be your friend when you won't give me one little shitty piece of your writing paper, and me good enough to lend you my grandma's shawl?'

'Take the filthy thing back,' said the duchess, throwing it on to the veranda floor. 'It only makes me itch.'

Another dismal silence fell. Peggy picked up the shawl and draped it round the old woman's shoulder. Then she looked through the railings to stare at the view she'd seen a thousand times before.

'To think I used to stay somewhere down there,' she said, 'and I don't even remember the name of the street. I expect it will be gone, though. It was during the war.'

'Ah yes, the war,' said the duchess, shifting restlessly in her seat. 'I remember the war. All those bombs falling. It was terrible.'

'And all those brick shelters. I remember refusing to go into them.'

'And all those American soldiers. Weren't they lovely?'

'I hated them,' said Peggy. 'They were ugly and loudmouthed.'

'Did you ever go out with any?'

'I didn't ever go out with any kind of soldier. I only had one boyfriend and that wasn't for long. Well, two if you count my boss.'

The duchess blinked as if she was on the point of a great discovery. 'Why, I believe I got married during the war,' she said. 'I distinctly remember going to the church, for some reason. It must have been that.'

'So you did have a husband?' said Peggy. 'Well, it's more than I did. Though they say you don't miss what you've never had. What I miss is dancing. I would love to have done a waltz round a floor in a dance-hall you sometimes see in old-fashioned films. I always thought I was cut out to be a dancer.'

The old woman stared at her blank-eyed as she went on, 'I remember tap dancing on the floor of our scullery. Being a stone floor it was good for that. I was only fourteen at the time and I thought one day –' She broke off. 'What's the point of talking about it. It doesn't do any good and anyway it won't be long now.'

'What won't?' said the duchess.

'Until they turf us out. I heard from the canteen woman this place is going to close soon and she's usually right about everything.'

'I don't understand,' said the duchess. 'How can they put me out if I've nowhere to go?'

'She said they'll give us a flat to share with someone. How would you like that?'

'I wouldn't like it at all,' said the duchess. 'I can't eat, I can't walk and now they tell me I've got dementia. How can I possibly share a flat?'

'Don't ask me,' said Peggy. 'Ask the sister. You know how she always listens.'

'I won't bother,' said the duchess, detecting a note of sarcasm in Peggy's tone. 'I know you're just trying to get me into trouble. I think you're a very wicked woman.'

Peggy had just left the shop to go home when she saw Boris cycling down the main street towards her. She might not have noticed him if it hadn't been for the rattling of his bicycle chain. The next moment it fell off and he was lying on the pavement beside her.

'Are you OK?' asked Peggy.

'Sure I'm OK.'

He scrambled up and gave the machine a kick. Peggy stared at him, mesmerised by his maturity. His face was thinner and paler and seemed to be all nose, yet he was still better looking than he used to be.

'Don't you remember me?' she said.

'Of course I do. You were the paper girl at Roper's.'

He knelt down to fix his chain. Peggy had the feeling of being dismissed. When she walked on he called out, 'Hold on a sec, I won't be long.'

She waited while he fiddled with the chain. When it was fixed she told him he had a grease mark on his cheek. He rubbed it off then stared at her in a puzzled way.

'You look different from when I last saw you,' he said.

'So do you.'

He stood frowning as if something worried him, then finally asked if she was doing anything in particular later on, and if not he'd like to take her out somewhere, but if she couldn't make it that was all right with him.

'I'm not doing anything,' she said.

'Then I'll meet you outside old Roper's shop at half-past seven and we could try that new ice-cream parlour that's opened up in the High Street.'

Peggy was affronted at Willie being called old but said, 'All right.'

There was no sign of Boris when she reached the shop, though his bicycle stood up against the building. Five minutes later he appeared from round the corner.

'I was just about to leave,' she said crossly.

'I was visiting Liza,' he explained.

'Liza?'

'Roper's wife, I thought I might as well pay her a visit while I was here. She was always good to me, not like him.'

Then he said he was going to put the bicycle behind the shop in case somebody stole it.

'Hurry up then,' said Peggy. 'I don't want to hang about here all night.'

She was worried that Willie might come out and see her with Boris, though she suspected he was more likely to be at the bowling club than with his wife.

'So where do you want to go?' Boris asked when he rejoined her.

'Didn't you say that new ice-cream shop?'

They sat inside the ice-cream parlour without speaking. Apart from two schoolboys giggling in a corner the place was empty. Peggy suspected they were giggling at her and Boris. Forcing herself to speak casually she asked him where he'd been since she last saw him.

'I'm in the cadets, training,' he said from the side of his mouth.

'Training for what?'

'The war. I'm going to join up when I'm old enough, like my brother.'

'Maybe the war will be over by then.'

'I hope not,' he said fiercely.

Another silence followed. Peggy's discomfort became acute when the schoolboys made explosive sounds behind their hands. In a distracted way she told Boris she now worked as Willie Roper's shop assistant.

'You do? I never would have thought that.'

'Why not?'

'It was bad enough delivering his papers.'

Peggy regarded him coldly. 'You never liked

him, did you? I suppose it was because he was a boss.'

'He was a creep as well. He should be in the war like other folk.'

Peggy sneered. 'First you call him old, and now you say he should be in the war. Make up your mind.'

'He's not too old to fight.'

Peggy finished her orange juice then stood up and said she was going.

'Hey, wait a minute!' he called after her. 'What's the matter?'

'It's the way you go on about Willie Roper. I would have thought you'd grown out of it. Why do you hate him so much?'

'I don't hate him. I don't even want to talk about him. I thought we might have gone into the amusement arcade, but –' He shrugged.

'All right, I'll come.'

'Listen, I can't stay at lunchtime. The gasman's coming to read the meter.'

'The gasman?'

Willie waited until the customer he'd been serving had left then he turned and told Peggy he'd never heard of a gasman working during his dinner break.

'He left us a note saying he'd call at that time. Maybe he thought it was the only time he'd catch us in.'

'Oh well, I suppose if that's it –' He sighed and walked into the back shop, his face petulant. Peggy felt guilty but had no intention of missing going to a special picture-house matinée with Boris at one-thirty. For the rest of the morning Willie went around with a scowl on his face.

'Cat got your tongue?' said one of the customers, who came in every morning for ten Woodbine, a paper, and a chat on either the weather or the war or both if he could manage it.

'It's the wife,' said Willie. 'Her arthritis is worse than usual. I doubt she'll have to go to hospital one of these days.'

'I'm sorry to hear that,' said the customer.

Later on when they were alone Peggy said, 'How do you mean she's getting worse? She was all right when I took up her bottle of sherry last Friday.'

'All I can say is that I couldn't get a wink of sleep for her moaning all through the night.'

Peggy's brain immediately became alert. 'How do you know that if you weren't sleeping in the same room?'

He regarded her with a wounded expression. 'Is that all that bothers you? She could be heard moaning throughout the building, if you must know.'

'I'm sorry. It's just that –'

'Just that what?'

'I get so fed up with all this secretiveness.'

'It's not any better for me,' he said, running

his finger up and down her bare arm. 'Must you really go home at lunch time?'

'You know I must,' she said, though part of her mind was already thinking she could wait on for half an hour at the least and it would still give her time to meet Boris. 'All right,' she said. 'I'll stay until one o'clock.'

When she got to the picture house, hot and flushed and ten minutes late, there was no sign of Boris or his bicycle. She waited for another three-quarters of an hour but he never appeared.

SIX

An incident took place in the ward that jolted
the patients out of their usual apathy, even those
who were practically comatose. For no apparent
reason a normally unobtrusive patient had thrust
a fork into the chest of a nurse during breakfast.
Luckily the fork was of the cheap variety and did
not much penetrate the skin, but it was enough
to create a high state of tension in the rest of the
staff. Five gathered round the erring patient and
whisked her so fast from the ward her feet scarcely
touched the ground.

'To think I've wanted to do something like
that for years,' said Peggy, doing a few steps of
the highland fling.

'Better watch or they'll have you off too,' said
the duchess.

'I'm sure I wouldn't mind. These jags they give
you are as good as a stiff drink. They put you out
like a light and that's something I could be doing

with nowadays. Even a couple of sleeping pills would be better than nothing.'

'I thought you'd stopped taking them because you wanted to write.'

'I'm fed up trying to write,' said Peggy. 'I can't get peace for people screaming and groaning. If it's not that they're snoring like troopers, you included. Anyway I've no paper left.'

'I don't snore,' said the duchess.

Peggy laughed. 'You snore worse than anybody. You snore so loud you waken yourself up.'

'You snore like an elephant,' said the old woman, determined not to be outdone.

Peggy shook her head, exasperated. 'The point I'm trying to make is if I don't get any peace to write and have no paper I might as well get doped up the same as everybody else. Understand?'

'I don't understand,' said the duchess. 'Everything you say is so totally absurd. I think you talk like that for spite.'

Then she began to chew on her lips and roll her eyes round her head like a frightened horse, which Peggy took to be a bad sign.

'Take it easy,' she said. 'The nurse will be along in a minute and you'll soon get your pills.'

'I'm not bothered about that,' snapped the duchess. 'What I want to know is where is my *True Romance*?'

'I told you before, I chucked it out. Anyway you don't want to read stuff like that at your age. You want to read something sensible.'

Without warning the old woman reached out and fastened her long bony fingers round Peggy's throat.

'Cunt!' she screamed. 'I'm going to kill you.'

A nurse rushed up and loosened her fingers by giving her what looked like a karate chop on the wrists.

'Is there something in here that's catching?' she said.

'She stole my *True Romance*,' sobbed the duchess.

'What's she talking about?' the nurse asked Peggy, who was feeling her throat tenderly with one hand.

'God knows,' said Peggy. 'She hasn't been herself lately.'

'I see,' said the nurse, looking from one to the other then crooking her finger in the old woman's direction. 'You come with me,' she said, 'and we'll soon sort everything out.'

'You know where my *True Romance* is?' said the duchess eagerly.

The nurse gave her a slight nod then took hold of her arm and led her out of the ward. Peggy watched them go with a slight twinge of guilt.

On Friday evening instead of fetching Mrs Roper's sherry she went straight to the amusement arcade hoping to see Boris again, not because she cared about him, she told herself, but because she wanted to be taken out.

The arcade was half empty. She saw at a glance he wasn't there. She hung around the entrance in the hope he'd show up. Two American soldiers walked past her. She'd heard that a squad of them were in town. One of them turned and said, 'Hello, doll.'

She blushed, intimidated by his bland good looks. He stopped and asked her what her name was. The other one kept walking.

'Peggy,' she said, thinking he might do instead of Boris.

'Peggy,' he said. 'That's a pretty name. You wanna come along with us?'

She was about to say yes, when the other soldier looked back and called out, 'C'mon man. Leave the kid alone.'

'But she wants to come along,' said his companion.

'No way. She's a sad apple. I can tell.'

'Sorry kid,' said the other one. He went up and joined his mate and they began to play the machines. Peggy left the arcade hurriedly with the words 'sad apple' ringing in her ears. At the last minute as she was about to go home she turned and went in the opposite direction to delay going in to an empty house.

'You're late,' said Mrs Roper, opening her door. 'Not that it matters. The shops are still open.'

Peggy followed her, thinking that contrary to what Willie had said his wife looked no worse than usual. Once inside the woman told her she was glad to see her. She couldn't have stood going without her sherry, especially on a Friday.

'Why on a Friday?' Peggy asked.

'I suppose it's because Friday is the night most people go out to enjoy themselves. Even Willie has his bowls.'

'I know what you mean,' said Peggy sadly.

'At your age?' asked Mrs Roper, surprised. Then she added looking into her face, 'Are you all right? You look pale.'

'I'm all right,' said Peggy, and burst into tears.

'Oh dear,' said Mrs Roper, handing her a handkerchief from somewhere within her cardigan. 'Would you like a cup of tea?'

Peggy shook her head, wishing she'd never come. She vowed to herself that she would never come again. The woman unnerved her.

'Or a glass of port? I might have some somewhere.'

'I don't want anything, I'm fine,' said Peggy. 'I'd better get to the shops before they close.'

'There's plenty of time,' said Mrs Roper, still staring intently into Peggy's face. Then she asked, 'Are you pregnant?'

Peggy gasped. 'What makes you say that?'

'I don't know,' said the woman. 'I suppose I get a feeling for these things.'

When she asked her gently who the father was, Peggy just managed to blurt out, 'A soldier,' before she fainted.

The duchess leaned over the side of her bed and jabbed Peggy with her walking-stick.

'Wake up.'

Peggy sat up, startled.

'What's happening?'

'Nothing. I only wanted to tell you I'm thinking of going on a hunger strike. It's the only way to get things done.'

Peggy looked down the ward where the patients were either asleep or comatose.

'You woke me up for that?' she said angrily. 'Just when I was getting to sleep?'

'Anyway it's time you were up,' said the old woman, poking her again. Peggy leapt out of bed, grabbed the stick and threw it on to the centre of the floor, wakening several patients who sat up startled.

'I've had enough of your carry-on,' said Peggy. 'Don't talk to me again.'

She walked out the ward and into the toilet area where she stood holding on to the rim of a wash-hand basin for support.

'Good God,' she said, catching sight of her face in the mirror. She'd never got used to how much like her mother's it had become. She could well imagine her saying, 'If only you had done what I told you everything would have been different.'

'Yes, Ma,' said Peggy. 'But how was I to know?'

At that moment a nurse came charging in.

'Oh there you are. I've been searching everywhere.' She peered in at an empty cubicle. 'Who were you talking to?'

'Nobody.'

'I heard voices.'

'That's because you've become like the rest of us.'

'Don't give me any of your lip,' said the nurse, gripping her hard on the fleshy part of her arm. 'You're in enough trouble as it is.'

'How's that?'

'You've been stealing the matron's writing paper. We found a bundle of it in your locker. I suppose you've been writing letters to the management complaining about the treatment. Well, if you think —'

'I'm writing a novel.'

'A novel?' said the nurse. She let out a peal of hysterical laughter then calmed down. 'What about?'

'Myself.'

'Yourself?'

'Yes, I've got plenty to write about with all the things that go on in here.'

'We all have plenty to write about,' said the nurse. 'I could write a few things about what goes on with the patients if I could be bothered.'

'But you can't be bothered,' said Peggy. 'That's the difference between you and me.'

The nurse opened her mouth to say something then shut it again, finally saying, 'I don't know why I'm listening to all this nonsense. Tell it to the matron when she sends for you, which she will be shortly. Meantime get back to bed and lay off the duchess. She doesn't know what she's doing any more.'

Wondering what had happened to Boris made Peggy vaguely unhappy. She couldn't resist asking about him amongst the paper boys. None had seen him, though most didn't know what he looked like anyway. Then one of them told her he'd heard that he'd been caught breaking into a shop and stealing cigarettes. She could hardly credit this. She was about to say it couldn't have been the same person when Willie Roper came into the back shop and said that if it was the Boris who'd worked in here he'd better not show his face and what was she wanting to know for.

'Somebody asked me for his address,' she said casually. 'You don't happen to know what it is?'

'I don't,' he said, giving her a glare which made her wonder if he'd seen them together on that last occasion. The rest of the morning he'd scarcely a word to say to her.

'Is there anything wrong?' she asked him when the shop was empty.

'Not really,' he said, and muttered something about having a lot on his mind.

'Is it something in connection with your wife?' she said, panicking in case Mrs Roper had mentioned she was going to have a baby.

'Worse than that,' he said. 'I'm expecting to get called up.'

'You are?' said Peggy, relieved. 'Aren't you too old?'

'I'm only thirty-seven, for Christ's sake.'

'I didn't mean that you're really old,' said Peggy, positive he'd told her he was forty-two. 'I only meant –'

'It's not that I'm scared to fight. It's the shop I'm thinking about and what's going to happen to Liza.'

'Liza?'

'You know how she depends on me. Who's going to look after her?'

Peggy turned away to serve a customer. Who's going to look after me, she thought, when I'm having your baby. She knew she'd have to tell him sometime, but there never seemed a right moment.

'I thought you were never going to serve me,' said the customer, a young and pretty woman who was flashing her teeth at Willie. Then she asked if there were any prunes in. She'd been hunting high and low for them.

'They'll be in soon,' said Willie, giving her back a wide admiring smile which made Peggy want to weep. She hadn't been getting very many smiles from him recently and it made her wonder if he no longer loved her.

SEVEN

The recreation room in the hospital was more like an old waiting room in a railway station, with torn brown leather chairs and a big ugly wooden table pushed against the wall. The only difference was a television set showing an old film with William Powell and Myrna Loy. The patients were either watching with rapt attention or were simply dazed. Peggy and the duchess sat further along the table playing cards.

'It's my turn to go first,' said the old woman.

'Are you sure?' said Peggy.

'I'm sure. You went first the last time.'

'I'm not sure I did,' said Peggy.

'Naturally,' said the duchess. 'I'd be surprised if you were sure of anything, considering the time you've been out for the count.'

'How long?'

'I should say about three days, off and on.'

Nothing was said for a while, then they began to

play cards, Peggy's face grim and the old woman's expressionless. After Peggy had won three games the duchess said she'd rather watch the film.

'Do what you like,' said Peggy, boxing the cards together and putting them in her pocket, then going over and taking a drink of water from a tap in the wash-hand basin. 'I can't get rid of this thirst,' she explained to the duchess, who asked her what she'd done to anger them. Peggy frowned.

'I can't remember exactly.' Then her face cleared. 'By God, I do. Didn't I go berserk when I discovered they had taken the manuscript out of my locker?' Bitterly she added, 'I suppose they'll have burned it by now.'

'Maybe not,' said the old woman weakly. Then she coughed once or twice before saying, 'If I tell you something, will you promise not to be angry?'

'How can I promise anything when I don't know what it is?'

'It was me who took it.'

'You took it?' said Peggy, her eyes bulging.

'I did it because you threw away my stick, remember. I was going to put it back but, when they came and searched your locker, I thought I might as well hold on to it for a time.'

'Why, you old cow.'

'At least it was safe with me. If I hadn't taken it it would have been in the furnace by now.'

Peggy thought for a bit. 'Maybe you were right

but I don't think I'll bother going on with it. I don't have any paper for a start.'

'I'll give you some of mine if you like.'

'That's good of you,' said Peggy, humble for once. 'But I've lost interest. Who would want to read about an old trout like me, in a nuthouse too, and not even mad enough to be interesting?'

'I think people might want to read it if you put some romance into it,' said the duchess. 'I mean if you wrote about falling in love with someone. Women always like to read about things like that.'

'For God's sake,' said Peggy, 'you should know by this time that there's no such thing as falling in love. It's only sex with a sugar coating round it. I once thought I was in love, but on looking back I can see it was nature's way of getting the female pregnant. We're just like animals, you know. Do you think *they* fall in love?'

'How can I tell what they're thinking?' said the duchess haughtily. 'But I'm quite sure they do in their own way.'

Her mouth closed firmly as she turned her attention to the film on the television. Peggy shook her head and went into a reverie which had nothing to do with her present circumstances.

One evening at tea-time Peggy's mother paused with her cup halfway up to her mouth and asked her daughter if she was correct in thinking that she'd put on weight recently.

'I'm pregnant,' said Peggy, the words out before she could stop them.

'Pregnant?' said her mother, putting her cup down and spilling tea all over the table.

'You don't have to worry,' said Peggy. 'It's my problem.'

Her mother stared at her in disbelief.

'Your problem?' she repeated. 'When I won't be able to face the neighbours or the people I work with or my friends? In fact I won't have any friends when this gets out. Who's the father?'

Peggy remained silent and her mother said, 'If you don't tell me I'll burn all your clothes.'

'Willie Roper.'

'My God,' said her mother, reeling back with her hand to her mouth. 'I might have known.'

'He doesn't know about it yet,' said Peggy, hardly thinking what she was saying, 'but anyway we're going to get married once he gets a divorce. He told me so.'

Her mother shrieked. 'Married to a man more than double your age who's already got a wife! It's disgusting.'

'I'm sorry,' said Peggy.

'Sorry?' said her mother. 'You don't know what sorry means. All your life you've been deaf to everything I've said. Now look what's happened. Pregnant at sixteen. If your father was alive this would never have happened. Oh Robert,' she moaned, 'if only you were here to help me.'

'Shush, Ma,' said Peggy. 'Willie's going to marry me. It's just a matter of time.'

'Time?' said her mother, as if she'd been reminded of something equally horrible. 'How far on are you?'

'Three or four months, I think.'

Her mother rose up, distraught. 'Then you've no time at all. Give me my coat. I'm going to see that bastard.'

'Wait a minute,' said Peggy, becoming equally distraught. 'He might not be in. He usually goes to the bowling green after his tea.'

'Then I'll talk to his wife. Wait until she hears about this. That'll give her something to think about. She always was stuck up, though I don't know why when she's only a cripple.'

But she must have thought better of it for she didn't make any move to get her coat. Staring at Peggy thoughtfully she said, 'Do you honestly think he'll divorce her to marry you?'

'He said he would,' said Peggy, unable to remember exactly what he'd said on the subject.

Her mother sat down looking more composed.

'Mind you,' she said, 'it wouldn't be such a bad idea if he did. That shop must be a regular gold mine.'

Peggy refrained from saying it was Willie's wife who owned the shop, lest it started another row.

'One way or another,' her mother added, 'he'll have to pay.'

'Pregnant?' said Willie Roper the following morning. 'Jesus Christ, since when?'

'I'm not sure. Three or four months.'

'In the name of God, why didn't you tell me sooner?'

'What difference would it have made?' said Peggy miserably. She'd been banking on him taking the news a lot better than this. She'd even thought he would have been pleased. Now she wondered how she could have been so stupid.

'Of course it would have made a difference. It would have been easier to get rid of it. As it is –' He broke off when a customer came in. 'Go into the back shop,' he hissed. 'I'll talk to you later.'

Five minutes later he came into the back shop and asked if anyone else knew.

'My mother,' she said, deciding not to say anything about his wife. He was in a bad enough mood.

'Your mother?' he said with a sharp intake of breath. 'What did she say?'

'I don't remember exactly. Something about making you pay.'

'She wants money from me. Is that it?'

Peggy became flustered. 'I don't know –'

'Well, she'd better not try to blackmail me if

that's what she's thinking or I'll get the police to her, and bugger the consequences.'

Peggy tried to keep the tears back, aware how easily her face got swollen nowadays.

'I don't care about my mother,' she said, 'so long as you still love me. That's all that counts.'

'Love,' he said dismissively. 'I don't think this is the time to talk about love. The important thing is that you mother doesn't get it into her head that she can get at me through my wife. I know for a fact Liza will stick by me. She always has.'

'Always has?' said Peggy in a hollow tone.

He glanced at her slyly. 'There have been others, you know.'

If Peggy's hand had been chopped off the statement couldn't have hurt her more. Her voice shook. 'Are you telling me that because you're angry with me?'

'No, it's true,' he said somewhat sheepishly. 'But I'm not so much angry with you as at myself for not taking precautions. Still,' he added in a more cheerful voice, 'it's no good crying over spilt milk. We'll just have to face up to the facts.'

His kindlier tone encouraged Peggy to come close to him so that they were almost touching.

'I don't care about the others,' she said. 'I'll always love you.'

Gently he pushed her away. 'I'll have to go back to the counter. There must be a pile of customers waiting. Stay there and I'll be back shortly.'

She waited for what seemed like ages. When she did finally look into the front shop he was leaning over the counter reading a newspaper. Blindly she reached for her coat and left through the back door.

While sitting on the veranda again Peggy said to her companion, 'Strangely enough, it's only when I'm writing that certain aspects of my life come back to me, otherwise my mind is usually a blank. For instance, it came to me just now there was a time during the war when I looked for him in pubs and railway stations, especially in railway stations. I always expected to find him coming off one of the trains with his uniform on. When I found out he'd got killed cycling in front of a bus I was almost glad. It saved me looking any more.'

The duchess said, 'I'm not sure who you're talking about.'

'That's because you never listen,' said Peggy. 'I was talking about Boris. Don't you remember I mentioned him earlier on?'

'Perhaps you did,' said the duchess. 'It's just that you keep jumping from one subject to the other. With all these men in your life it's a wonder you never contracted a disease.'

'Sorry,' said Peggy, 'but I only had two men in my life who meant anything to me, and you couldn't really count Boris as he was only a childhood sweetheart.'

'They do say that disease was caught mainly in the foreign brothels,' said the duchess, who hadn't been listening. 'I recall my husband mentioning this. Not that he went into any great detail, knowing how it would upset me. He was a very considerate man.'

'I'm sure he was,' said Peggy, 'though it's a pity he never visited you all the time you were in here.'

'Indeed,' said the old woman peevishly. 'But then he could have died, couldn't he? It was a long time ago.'

Peggy stuffed the writing pad she'd been reading from into her pocket. 'I don't think I'll write any more. My mind's gone blank.'

For some reason this seemed to anger the duchess. 'Give me that paper back. There's no use in having it if you're not going to use it.'

'Why, you old devil, you insisted I take it and it isn't even yours if you remember. You told me you stole it from that new patient, remember?'

The duchess blinked rapidly. 'I don't recall saying that.'

'Well, you did. Do you want me to go and tell her?'

'Don't bother. It will only cause trouble. Keep the paper if it means all that much to you.'

'I don't know that I want it,' said Peggy. 'There's not much point in writing anything if you're not going to listen. You're the only audience I've got.'

'But I will listen,' said the duchess eagerly. 'Please tell me about the man who was killed in the war. Were you very fond of him? I'm really interested.'

'I don't want to talk about it,' said Peggy. 'I'm going in now.'

'Please don't go,' said the duchess. 'I know I'm always saying the wrong thing, but I am interested in what you write, especially now that I haven't got anything else to read.'

'There you go again,' said Peggy. 'I suppose if you had something else to read you wouldn't be interested. Is that it?'

'No, it isn't,' said the old woman. She began to cry weakly. 'It's just that I don't feel well and I think I'm going to die.'

'Oh yeah,' said Peggy, with a sardonic smile. 'Well, before you die listen to this.'

She took out the pad from her pocket and began to read aloud.

'I've had a long discussion with Willie Roper,' said Peggy's mother, 'and we've come to an agreement. You'd better understand that you can't keep it, and you'll have to stay indoors until arrangements can be made.'

'What's going to happen?' said Peggy, guessing what the answer would be.

'Adoption,' said her mother, smiling encouragingly. 'It's the only way. Between the money

I've got left from your father's insurance and what Willie is putting towards it, we'll be able to get you into a place three months before you're due, then when the baby is born it will be handed over to a nice couple who'll give it a home. And I hope you appreciate what we are doing for you,' she added earnestly.

'I'm not having the baby adopted,' said Peggy.

'You'll do as you're told.'

'It's my baby,' said Peggy. 'You can't make me.'

'Look,' said her mother, trying a softer approach, 'you've got your whole life in front of you. You don't want to start it as the mother of a bastard child.'

'I'm not going to listen to you,' said Peggy. 'I'm going to see Willie Roper for myself and hear what he says.'

'I told you. He wants it adopted. He's willing to pay,' said her mother.

'I want to hear him say it then.'

'You can't leave the house,' her mother shrieked. 'People will notice that you've put on weight as well as those black shadows under your eyes.'

Peggy walked out while she was still shouting.

'Your mother is right,' said Willie, ushering her into the back shop. 'You shouldn't come here in that state. It'll look suspicious if Liza walks in and catches us. She's been acting very funny lately. I'm just hoping it's her time of life.'

'I thought you said she was practically dying.'

'Not so much dying as chronically ill. And why did you tell her you were pregnant and the father was a soldier? She didn't have to know anything.'

'She guessed I was pregnant and I had to tell her something, didn't I?'

'Yes, but why a soldier?' He gave her a sidelong glance. 'Unless it's true.'

'Of course it isn't,' she cried. 'I've never been with anybody but you.'

'All right, keep your voice down,' he said. 'The customers might hear.'

'Is that all you care about, your customers?' she said bitterly.

'Now you know that's not true,' he said, putting his arm round her shoulder. 'It's you I'm concerned about. Can't you see that?'

She moved away from him and said she was going to keep the baby, no matter what. His face hardened.

'If you do I'll wash my hands of you altogether and God knows what will happen to you. Society doesn't look kindly on young girls who have illegitimate children. God knows, I didn't mean you to have a child but now that it's happened we can only do our best to rectify the situation. The only other alternative is an abortion which could be messy and dangerous. So go home and think about it.'

She turned and left the shop, his words ringing in her ears like a death knell.

EIGHT

'Wake up, lazy-bones, and get up so that I can make the bed,' said the nurse, towering over the duchess who lay so small and thin under the covers that she scarcely ruffled them.

The old woman opened her eyes and said, 'Leave me alone. Can't you let me die in peace?'

'You can die in peace after I make the bed,' said the nurse, hauling at the blankets, then sniffing the air. 'Why, I do believe you've wet it again. I can smell it from here.'

The duchess swung her thin legs on to the floor.

'It's not my fault that I've a weak bladder,' she said piteously.

'It's not a weak bladder,' said the nurse, heaving the blankets on to the floor. 'You just can't be bothered to get up. That's what it is.' She stared at the offending sheet. 'Look at that. Damned well soaking and it was only changed yesterday.'

Swaying like a reed in the wind the duchess said, 'You haven't by any chance seen my slippers? I need the toilet.'

Not deigning to answer her the nurse called on Peggy who was helping to serve the porridge.

'What's she done this time?' said Peggy.

'Get her out of here,' said the nurse. 'She wants to go to the toilet. As if it's not enough that she'd already wet the bed.'

'I want my slippers,' said the duchess querulously.

'Look under the bed,' said Peggy.

Once out in the corridor Peggy asked the duchess if she couldn't walk any faster as she didn't want her porridge to get cold.

'It's my heart,' said the duchess. 'It beats too fast and I can't take much more of the aggravation these nurses are giving me.'

Inside the toilet cubicle she began to complain that she was having difficulty moving her bowels. Peggy turned on the tap to avoid hearing this, while trying not to look in the mirror in case she saw her mother's face again. At last the old woman came from the cubicle explaining that she hadn't made her will and must do so soon or the estate would go to a distant relative she hardly knew.

'That's right,' said Peggy. 'One of those rich bastards in Australia with a sheep farm.'

'How did you know?' said the duchess, wiping her perfectly dry hands on a towel.

'It usually happens that way, doesn't it?'

'I know what I'll do,' said the duchess. 'I'll leave everything to the hospital. The money can be used to build a new wing, and there might be enough left over to put a plaque up with my name on it.'

Peggy's mouth fell open. Even in fantasy the idea was outrageous.

'You'd leave your money to the people who run this horror camp for the sake of having your name on a plaque?'

'Well, I've no one else to leave it to,' said the old woman huffily.

'What about me?' said Peggy. 'Or that husband you're always talking about?'

The old woman regarded her steadily. 'Why, my dear, I don't have a husband, and never had. You should know that by this time.'

Peggy rolled her eyes in mock despair. 'That's right. I keep forgetting nothing is real with you. You could be Alice in Wonderland and me the White Rabbit for all you know.'

During the day Peggy had to stay indoors. When it was dark she walked the back streets to get some fresh air, wearing a slack coat to hide her figure, though there was little to hide at this stage. When she pointed this out her mother said, 'But you can't be too careful.'

The months dragged on until the time came for Peggy to go to the home.

'I've spoken to the woman on the phone,' said her mother. 'She sounds very nice. All she requires of you is to do a little light housework, nothing strenuous.'

'Will I be the only one there?' Peggy asked, resolving to run away at the first opportunity.

'Of course not,' said her mother. 'There's more than you gets into this kind of mess, but mind you, they're usually a lot older, so thank your lucky stars you've been accepted. At your age they could have turned you down.'

'I wish they had,' said Peggy under her breath.

The evening before she left she wrote a letter to Willie Roper informing him about her departure and saying that if he didn't help her to keep the baby she was going to tell his wife. She was sealing the envelope and wondering how she could get a stamp when her mother came in to the room shouting at the top of her voice that she'd just heard Willie Roper had been called up, which would likely mean that they wouldn't get a penny out of him if he was in the army.

'Does that mean I don't have to go to this home?' said Peggy.

'Oh no, you're going,' said her mother, 'even if it leaves me a pauper. I'm not going to have any bastard child in my house.'

The journey in the tramcar took an hour, during which Peggy stared blankly out the window while her mother looked stonily ahead.

She'd hardly spoken a word to her daughter except to say how Willie Roper had skedaddled off to the war to avoid paying out the money and that she blamed Peggy for everything.

The big house might have been grand in its day but had a neglected air. Bushes in the front garden had been allowed to grow wild and the path to the door was covered in weeds. The woman who opened it was tall with thick wiry hair and protuberant eyes. She introduced herself as Lily and led them to a clean but drab room with faded linoleum, two single beds, a wardrobe and a wash-hand basin with a pail under it. Peggy wondered about that pail.

'Very nice,' said Peggy's mother with a fulsome smile.

'We do our best,' said Lily, then told Peggy, 'take your coat off and hang it in the wardrobe with your other stuff.'

She went out with Peggy's mother and closed the door, leaving her inside. Peggy was hanging up her things when there was a knock and a voice said, 'Can I come in?'

Peggy turned to see a woman with short red hair, neither young nor old-looking, her face a mass of freckles.

'I'm Annie,' she said.

Peggy was reassured by the woman's plain but friendly features.

'And I'm Peggy,' she said. 'Have you come to show me what to do?'

'Not yet,' said Annie. 'I came to let you know tea is at six and I'll give you a call then.'

Peggy was dismayed to learn she would have to wait in the room for all that time.

'Is there no heating?' she asked.

'There's an electric fire there,' said Annie, pointing to a space between the beds. 'We're not supposed to use it through the day. If Lily comes in don't tell her I told you about it.'

Peggy nodded. Her feet were numb. At that moment an electric fire was her idea of heaven.

'Am I sharing this room with you?'

'No, I'm in another room,' said Annie. 'There's nobody else in here but yourself, but you never know who's going to come in beside you. It's that kind of place.'

She looked at Peggy curiously.

'You're in for three months, I hear.'

'At least that,' said Peggy with a tremor in her voice.

'I know it will seem bad at first,' said Annie, 'but you'll get used to it. I've been here for five months.'

'That long?' said Peggy, surprised. 'Isn't your baby adopted yet?'

'Two months ago,' said Annie, and fell silent. Then she said that she'd only stayed on to give

Lily a hand until she got a job that suited her. 'I prefer cleaning houses,' she added.

Peggy found it hard to believe anybody would want to stay on any longer than was necessary.

'That woman in charge, Lily, what's she like?'

'She's not bad if you take her the right way.'

'I see,' said Peggy, wondering what the right way was. She pointed to the pail and asked what it was for.

'It's for when we need the lavvy,' said Annie. 'We're not allowed to use the proper lavvy in case of germs. The midwife is very particular about germs.'

'But I can't use a pail,' said Peggy, aghast. 'I'll die if I have to.'

'Well, you'll just have to,' said Annie. 'It's one of the rules.' She regarded Peggy with concern, then said, 'I must go now or else she'll be wondering where I am.'

Peggy had used up all her writing paper and, being possessed by the urge to set down her life story before she lost the thread of it, she asked the night nurse in the ward if she could possibly get her a jotter and she'd pay for it out of her meagre allowance. The nurse raised one eyebrow and said she would see. Peggy sensed by her tone she'd either forget or had no intention of seeing, so when the duchess shuffled down the ward to find out what was going on at the bottom she began to search in the old woman's locker on the off-chance of finding something to write upon, even if it was only a piece of toilet roll.

For her part the duchess had stopped to watch a group of patients playing gin rummy round a patient's bed, which wasn't allowed, but the night nurse was quite often out of the ward either having a smoke or a blether. The game reminded the duchess of the times when she was a young girl and people came to the house on Sundays to play cards with her parents. Strangely she couldn't remember her parents too much and hardly anything else about her childhood or even her later years. Sometimes she had the impression she'd been born an old woman.

One of the card players beckoned her over and whispered something in her ear, which caused her to turn round and shuffle back up the ward tapping her stick as she went.

'What are you doing?' she said to Peggy who was hunkered down on her knees searching the back of the old woman's locker, her imperial mints rolling all over the floor.

'Looking for something to write on,' said Peggy. 'What do you think?'

'How dare you!' said the duchess, poking Peggy in the back with her stick.

Peggy immediately rose up and took the stick

off her then strode out on to the veranda. A nurse came at her back.

'I hope you're not going to do anything foolish,' she said.

Peggy pointed towards the duchess who was wringing her hands and giving a good impression of someone severely demented.

'She attacked me with this stick and it's not the first time, so I'm going to get rid of it.'

'Over the veranda?' said the nurse.

'Where else?'

'Tell me,' said the nurse, squeezing the soft part of Peggy's arm in a vice-like grip, 'do you often throw things over the veranda?'

Peggy clamped her lips together as the nurse escorted her up the ward, passing the duchess who was clawing at her hair, then out into the small room with no windows and no furniture except for a medicine chest on the wall. After locking the door she slapped Peggy hard on each cheek and asked her what was bothering her.

'Nothing,' said Peggy. 'I only wanted paper to write on and I thought she had some in her locker.'

'So you thought you'd the right to help yourself to it.'

'She said I could.'

'Roll up your sleeve,' said the nurse. 'Let's see what your blood pressure's like.'

Before Peggy could refuse she'd unlocked the

medicine chest from which she brought out a syringe then stuck it into Peggy's arm saying, 'This is for your own good.'

Peggy slept all the next day until tea-time. When she woke up there were two jotters on top of her locker. The duchess called from the chair at her bedside, 'Look what the nice nurse left you after I told her you were writing a novel.'

'Fuck you and the nice nurse,' said Peggy. 'And don't do me any favours in future. I was in the punishment room because of you.'

'You brought it upon yourself,' said the duchess. She added, 'I've been reading more of your story while you were sleeping. It's actually quite interesting in parts.'

Peggy touched an eye that was turning black. 'To think you've been as crazy as a coot for the past two days and now you're acting as if butter wouldn't melt in your mouth. What's the matter with you?'

The duchess came over and whispered, 'I want you to know that there's not a soul in this ward I'd talk to except yourself. They're all too ignorant. At least I can appreciate what you're trying to do. They wouldn't have a clue.'

'Is that right?' said Peggy. 'Well, I won't be doing any writing tonight. My head feels like it's crawling with worms.'

'Never mind,' said the duchess. 'We'll sit out

on the veranda later on and watch the street
lights. We might see that man again. What's
his name?'

'I don't know,' said Peggy.

NINE

Peggy was on her way back from the dairy with a shopping bag containing six pints of milk over each arm.

'The even weight should balance you up nicely,' Lily had said before Peggy set off. In theory this might have been true but in practice her arms felt as if they were being wrenched out of their sockets. She stopped halfway to unbutton her once slack coat that was now so tight it was making her sweat. Resisting the impulse to stop for longer she carried on into the lane that led to the back of the house. She'd been warned not to come in the front door in case the sight of a pregnant woman gave the place a bad name.

Annie opened the door, shaking her head. Needlessly she said, 'You shouldn't be lugging all that weight in your condition,' since they both knew Peggy had no choice in the matter. In the big kitchen Lily was stirring a pot of porridge on the kitchen range. She ordered a plate to be put out for the new client who had come in the previous night.

'Is that who it was. I thought I heard something,' said Annie.

'Yes, at half-past ten,' said Lily. 'Some people have no consideration.'

At that point a woman entered in an advanced state of pregnancy and stared around as if wondering if she'd come to the right place.

'Sit down, please,' said Lily, pointing to the table, and then placing a bowl of porridge in front of her. The woman said she didn't eat porridge since it made her sick just to look at it.

'You won't get anything else,' said Lily.

'Not even a cup of tea?' said the woman.

'Not at the moment. You'll have to wait.'

'I'll wait,' said the woman. She took out a cigarette from a packet she'd been holding in her hand and asked if anyone had a match.

'Smoking?' said Lily, scandalised. 'And you expecting any minute.'

'I've been smoking for nine months,' said the woman. 'It's a bit late to start worrying about it now.'

'Well, you still want to chuck it,' said Lily. 'It's a filthy habit and I'm not having you smoking in my kitchen.'

Peggy and Annie listened to the conversation with interest. It was a change from the usual silence if Lily was in the kitchen. Then a bell rang which meant the midwife wanted her.

'Who does that cow think she is?' said the woman when Lily had gone. 'She needn't tell me what to do. I paid good money to come here.'

'She's not that bad,' said Annie. 'Her bark's worse than her bite.'

'Well, if that's her bark I wouldn't like to see her bite,' said the woman, tearing a strip off the newspaper and sticking it in the fire to light her cigarette. 'By the way,' she added, 'my name's Cathy. What's yours?'

'I'm Peggy.'

Annie frowned as she stared at the torn newspaper. 'She'll have something to say about that.'

'She can say what she likes,' said Cathy. 'I hardly think she'll fling me out.' She added, 'Is there any chance of getting a cup of tea now she's gone?'

Annie put on the kettle and said they might as well all have a cup of tea. Peggy then told Cathy she'd been here for two months and would likely be here for another two.

'You've got my sympathy,' said Cathy. 'I couldn't stick this place for more than a day. I'm only in here to have the kid and then I'm off.' She stared at Peggy curiously. 'Aren't you a bit young to be having a kid? You don't look more than fourteen.'

'I'm sixteen.'

'You're still too young at sixteen. Was it some

old married man that did it? It's usually the case now that all the young men are being called up.'

'We don't discuss our personal affairs in here,' said Annie stiffly.

'Pardon me,' said Cathy, after taking a long tense pull at her cigarette. 'I don't care who knows mine. I'm in here to have a kid for my sister since she can't have one herself.'

'That's good of you,' said Annie. 'I know I wouldn't like going through all the bother for somebody else, even my sister.'

'Well, you see,' said Cathy, 'the man involved was her husband and when she discovered I was having his kid she thought it best to keep it in the family.'

'I see,' said Annie a trifle coldly, while Peggy tried to figure it all out.

Lily came in and sniffed the air suspiciously, but said nothing. She told Peggy to polish the furniture in the front room after she'd washed the dishes, and Annie to change the beds in the rooms that were not being used.

'And you,' she said to Cathy, 'bring in coal for the fire. You'll get it in the bunker outside.'

Cathy said she'd no intention of doing anything, she hadn't come here to be a servant. Besides, she thought she was going into labour since she was having pains in her back. Lily said in that case she'd better go to her room and stay there until the midwife came.

'But it's freezing in there,' said Cathy. 'I'll catch my death, sure as God.'

Lily opened the kitchen door wide and beckoned her to leave.

'I'm afraid we can't have you in the kitchen if you're in labour. So please go or I'll have to remove you by force.'

'Oh no you don't,' said Cathy. 'I'm getting out of this dump and I want my money back.'

'Dear me, no,' said Lily. 'You can't have it back. You signed an agreement.'

'What agreement?' said Cathy. Then she went chalk white and sank into a chair. 'Jesus Christ, I believe I am in labour. I've just had one hell of a pain.'

'I thought you might be,' said Lily. 'Come along and I'll fetch the nurse.'

They both left the kitchen with Cathy hunched and shaking all over.

'I doubt we'll see her again,' said Annie.

'But she's right,' said Peggy. 'Why does Lily treat us like hired help when we're paying for it?'

'Because it's cheaper than some of the other places. It saves us money and them as well if they get their help for nothing.'

'Like you and me.'

'Exactly,' said Annie. 'There's no union rules here.'

'I suppose not,' said Peggy, regretting that she wouldn't see Cathy again. Annie was all right, but too meek and mild and always sided with Lily.

During the early hours of the morning the duchess called out for a bedpan, which request was ignored until Peggy stamped out the ward and down the corridor and into the room where all the bedpans were kept in neat rows.

'Didn't you hear old Violet shouting?' she asked two nurses who had been talking to each other in a desultory manner. They gave her a blank stare and walked away.

'Never mind,' Peggy called after them. 'I see you're busy.'

Back in the ward she discovered the old woman sitting up in a lop-sided manner with her mouth hanging open.

'Here's your bedpan,' said Peggy, shoving it into her face, but the old woman didn't move a muscle and when Peggy shook her lightly on the shoulder she toppled over.

'Nurse,' called Peggy, running out of the ward.

Ten minutes later a nurse came through to check the duchess's pulse and finished up sending for the sister who took one look at the patient and arranged for a screen to be put round her bed. It didn't stop Peggy from shouting over it that if they'd got the old woman a bedpan sooner she'd probably have been OK.

'If you don't shut your mouth I'll shift you to

B ward among the advanced cases,' said the sister, coming out from the screen. 'Meanwhile go and take a bath so that we may be allowed to give this patient proper treatment.'

When Peggy returned half an hour later the duchess and her bed were gone. Later in the morning she was told by one of the friendlier nurses that she might not last the day.

'I bet she won't,' said Peggy angrily. 'They'll have been giving her one of those lethal injections to finish her off.'

'Get that woman out of here,' said the matron, who happened to come into the ward to do her morning rounds, accompanied by two orderlies for protection, and an elderly male doctor who appeared to be half asleep. Once again Peggy was locked up in the small padded room, but this time without the injection. When she got out next morning she went to the veranda to get some fresh air and was in time to see a coffin being taken to a limousine by two men in bowler hats. She guessed the coffin was the duchess's.

'Coo-ee,' she shouted, in the hope the men would be startled enough to drop it. It wouldn't do the duchess any harm if she fell out in front of the traffic but it wouldn't look so good for the hospital. However they didn't turn as much as a hair, not even when she added, 'Murderers.'

Back in the ward she took from under her vest the jotter and pencil she always kept and read aloud the chapter she had written in the punishment room.

Every Saturday Peggy's mother came to the home and paid the weekly fee, then Peggy accompanied her back to the tram stop by way of a park with a pond where children threw bread to the ducks. Peggy always wished she had sneaked some bread out. It would have been a cheerful thing, feeding the ducks, but by the time she'd finished all her chores and got herself ready she'd forgotten about the bread. In any case her mother was always in a hurry, though whatever for Peggy couldn't think.

'I wish you'd keep up with me,' her mother was now saying. 'My feet are freezing with having to walk so slow.'

'I'm going as fast as I can,' said Peggy. To point out that her increasing weight was holding her back would only have provoked her mother into making some kind of bitter comment. She was never encouraged to speak about her condition. Therefore it was a shock when she said, 'It won't be long now until the little bastard's born and I won't have to come here and pay a third of my wages to that greedy bitch, and as well as that I won't have to tell any more lies when people ask about you.'

'I'm sorry,' said Peggy.

'And so you should be. Do you know some

parents would have put their daughters in an asylum for what you've done. Think yourself lucky that I didn't.'

'I do.'

'Another thing, when this is over you'll be taking a job in an office even if it's only to make the tea and you'll stay away as far as possible from Willie Roper's shop.'

'I thought he was in the army,' said Peggy, startled at the mention of his name.

'So did I but I heard he got a discharge on account of having varicose veins or something equally ridiculous. And it appears his wife is dying, and his business is not doing so good. If it had been I would have been on to him like a shot for the money he owes me, but I suppose you can't get blood out of a stone.'

Peggy had a fleeting recollection of Mrs Roper thrusting a book into her hand and telling her a good book helps you to understand yourself as well as others. Tears of sorrow and shame came into her eyes. She gave an involuntary sob.

'What's the matter with you?' said her mother. 'I hope you're not thinking of that Willie Roper.'

'If you must know I wish I was dying.'

'Well, you'd better not be. I've enough to contend with.'

They left the park and came out into a short street of tenement buildings with a public house at the end of it.

'I think I'll nip in for a small port while I'm waiting for the tram,' said her mother. 'I need something to buck me up after all this −' Her voice broke off as though there was no need to explain.

'Yes, you should,' said Peggy, and was going to add, 'See you next Saturday,' but her mother had disappeared through the swing doors.

'I'll be leaving at the end of the week. I've got a job,' Annie whispered, though there were only she and Peggy in the kitchen. For the past few days there had been no clients. Lily had explained they were taking in no one else meanwhile, since the midwife wanted a break over Christmas.

'That means I'll be here on my own,' said Peggy in a tone of dread.

'Surely you can put up with that? You don't have long to go.'

'How do I know how long I've got after the birth?' said Peggy. 'And it's plain that Lily hates me. It's going to be worse if you're not here.'

'She doesn't hate you. It's only her manner.'

Peggy began to cry. 'I know she hates me. If you go I'll kill myself.'

'For goodness sake, stop it,' said Annie. 'You are making me feel bad and I thought you would have been glad for my sake. After all, I've been here for months on end.'

Peggy wiped her eyes on her sleeve.

'I am glad for you. It's just that I'm going to miss you terribly. So what kind of a job is it?'

'It's cleaning a dentist's surgery,' said Annie. 'I had a notion of working in a shop, but I'm no good at counting. Cleaning's all I know.'

'It's easy to work in a shop,' said Peggy with a touch of scorn. 'I did.'

'So you did,' said Annie, 'and look what happened.'

Peggy bit back an angry retort and said instead, 'My mother's almost fifty and she works in a munitions factory. You should try that. It's more money.'

'So I should,' said Annie in a sarcastic voice. She went over to the sink and filled a basin with water. 'If we don't get a move on we'll both be getting it in the neck from you know who and I don't want to annoy her in case she doesn't give me a reference.'

So much for sticking in with Lily, thought Peggy. She began to wipe the table while Annie went down on her knees to wash the floor. Nothing was said as they worked, until Peggy was struck by a notion. She asked Annie if she ever regretted having her baby adopted.

'What a question!' said Annie, squinting up at her. 'What brought that on?'

'I only wondered, because I'm sure I would. In fact when the time comes I'm going to keep my baby.'

'You think so?' said Annie in a sneering sort of way, which made Peggy wish she hadn't said anything. Changing the subject she added, 'What's the midwife like, I mean when you're in labour? I hope she's not anything like Lily.'

'She does what she has to do, if that's what you're asking.'

'I see,' said Peggy, not reassured by this statement. The one time she'd seen the midwife was when she was standing in the doorway of the kitchen watching them while they cleaned up. She was fat all over with piggy eyes and bare arms that looked as strong as a man's.

'Is there anything else you want to know?' said Annie, rising to her feet with a scowl.

'No, nothing,' said Peggy, now almost in tears at the way Annie spoke. 'I didn't mean to annoy you,' she added. 'It's just that I feel so miserable about you going.'

Annie's face softened. 'You didn't annoy me. Just don't be too upset, that's all. It's not as if I won't be in touch. I'll write to you as soon as I'm settled.'

'That'll be great,' said Peggy, forcing a smile and knowing it would be most unlikely. In her place she would have wanted to forget everything connected with the home.

TEN

'Don't make so much noise,' said the midwife, bending over Peggy who was screaming with pain. 'You're not co-operating. Press when I tell you.'

Peggy scarcely heard her. She thought she was going to die.

'And keep on pressing until I tell you to stop, otherwise I'll have to use forceps and I don't think you'll like that.'

The word 'forceps' galvanised Peggy into giving one almighty push and the baby's head appeared.

'Now press again,' said the midwife.

Peggy thought definitely she was going to die. She screamed and pressed at the same time until the rest of the baby emerged. Then she passed out and woke up in a different room with a black dog at her feet which she took to mean she'd died and gone to hell. Lily entered with a bundle in her arms.

'You've got a fine boy,' she said, 'and now you'll have to feed him.'

'I'm too tired,' said Peggy, only wanting to return to oblivion and never waken up again.

'You'll feed him whether you're tired or not,' said Lily, thrusting the child into Peggy's arms so that she was forced to look at him. He didn't look human, she thought, more like a fledgling with his wrinkled skin and beaky nose.

'I've no milk,' she said.

'You'll have milk,' said Lily. 'Put him on your right nipple for five minutes then change to your left.'

Peggy fumbled at the buttons on her nightdress, affronted at having to expose her chest to Lily's grim gaze. It was painful at first when the infant began to suck. After a few minutes the pain eased off.

'Didn't I say you had milk?' said Lily.

Peggy asked what she was to do with him when he'd had enough.

'Keep him beside you. I'll bring in a cot.'

'Is he to be with me all the time?'

'Oh yes,' said Lily. 'Up until the time he's to be adopted, and as for that dog,' she added, pointing to the animal who had made itself comfortable at the bottom of the bed, 'keep him out of here. He's supposed to be guarding the house.'

The days passed slowly and Peggy never left the room except to go to the toilet. Being no longer pregnant she didn't have to use the pail. All the other rooms in the house were locked including the kitchen and Lily came in only twice a day to leave Peggy a meal and make sure the infant was being fed and changed properly.

'We don't want you neglecting him,' she said. 'That child's valuable.'

Although more or less a prisoner Peggy wasn't too unhappy. The baby took up all her time and during the night she took him into bed beside her, while the dog lay at the bottom. It was a cosy arrangement and although she still planned to escape with the baby the sameness of the everyday routine lulled her into a false sense of security.

One morning Lily arrived with the breakfast, toast and a boiled egg, porridge being too much trouble to make for one, and asked her if she had a name for the child.

'Robert,' said Peggy. Then after a slight hesitation, 'It's my da's.'

She would have liked to call him William but it didn't seem appropriate when his father would never know him.

Lily nodded. 'It's only for the records. Whoever adopts him will likely change it.'

Peggy's heart sank. She'd have to make her getaway soon but how could she when the front door was always locked from the outside? And if she did manage to escape where would she go?

'Somebody has sent you a present,' said Lily, arriving on Christmas Day with a small parcel and throwing it on to the bed. For a wild moment Peggy thought it might be from Willie Roper, but on opening it she discovered it was from her mother, a red headscarf with black dots.

'Very nice,' said Lily sarcastically. 'I'm sure it must have cost a fortune.'

Peggy felt insulted on her mother's behalf. 'She can't afford much when she's got to pay for me,' she said.

'Maybe, but she could have at least visited you, considering it's Christmas, instead of sending it on.'

Peggy dropped her eyes. She wasn't going to run down her mother to this woman. Lily shrugged.

'Still, I dare say it's none of my business. How about a slice of apple crumble with your dinner tonight? Will that make you feel any better?'

Peggy nodded to convey that it would, then encouraged by Lily's unusually sympathetic tone she asked if she could go outside for a walk.

'Outside?' said Lily, flabbergasted. 'And who's going to look after the baby?'

'I thought you might,' said Peggy, not daring to look at her in case she went into a rage.

Surprisingly she agreed. 'Only for half an hour,' she said, adding that she'd enough to do without looking after somebody else's child.

'Do you think I could have some bread to feed the ducks?' said Peggy. 'I've always wanted to feed them and the pond's not far.'

'Dear Christ, whatever next,' said Lily. She stamped out of the room then came back with some bread in a poke. 'Mind,' she said, 'no more than half an hour.'

Peggy walked around the pond, with the ducks following her, glad there was no one else to see her in the slack coat. Twice she went round the pond with the ducks at her back until the bread was finished.

'No more,' she said, shooing them away, then headed back towards the house, positive she hadn't been gone for as much as half an hour, but somehow she had the feeling her child was crying out for her. She began to run.

Lily was waiting for her in the hallway.

'Thank God you're back,' she said. 'A couple came about the baby around twenty minutes ago and as you weren't in they said they'd come back tomorrow. I knew I shouldn't have let you go out.'

The matron sat staring at the folder in front of her then finally looked up at Peggy and said, 'I want you to know you're going to be discharged soon. As to the date I cannot say exactly –' Then she stopped, struck by Peggy's blank face. 'Did you hear what I said?'

Peggy nodded her head.

'Well, aren't you pleased?'

'Not particularly.'

The matron looked surprised.

'Don't you want to leave?'

Peggy shook her head.

'For goodness sake, why not?'

'I want to stay and finish my writing.'

'Your writing?' said the matron, peering at the pages inside the folder. 'There is no mention of writing in here.'

'I can't help that,' said Peggy. 'I'm writing a novel and I don't want to be distracted from it. Being discharged would distract me so much I might not be able to continue.'

The matron looked annoyed.

'It's not up to you to decide whether you leave or not. This isn't a holiday camp where one can lounge about writing novels, and I'm sure you'll have fewer distractions in a place of your own than in here.'

When Peggy remained silent the matron said, 'Perhaps you're distracted already by the death of your friend?'

'What friend?'

'Why, old Mrs Smith, better known as the duchess. She was your friend, wasn't she?'

'She was in no condition to be anybody's friend,' said Peggy.

'But still you must miss her. Anyway,' she added impatiently, 'whether you like it or not you're going to be discharged into a nice little flat where I'm sure you'll be very happy and you'll be able to come and go as you please, provided you conform to the rules.'

'So there are rules?'

'Naturally. We must all abide by rules.'

'Is that so,' said Peggy, holding the matron's gaze steadily. 'What about my pills?'

'Your pills?'

'If I don't get them I'm liable to break the rules.'

'But you don't need pills,' said the matron. 'That's why we're sending you out. You're cured.'

Peggy leaned forward and hissed into the matron's face, 'I'm no more cured than you are.'

Immediately the matron put her finger on a bell under her desk and an orderly appeared.

'Everything all right?' the orderly asked, looking from the matron to Peggy then back again.

'Everything's fine,' said the matron. 'Just take this patient away and give her the usual pills. We'll get no peace otherwise.'

Peggy's mother bought her a coat two days previous to the adoption.

'We can't have you coming home like a tramp,' she'd said. 'I've told everyone you were working in London, so remember, if anyone asks you where you've been –'

'I'll remember,' Peggy said. At the last minute she pleaded with her mother to let her keep the baby – they could say she'd got married in London and her husband was away to the war. Her mother became so angry that she slapped Peggy's face saying, 'You must be joking.'

It was then Peggy gave up all hope of a last-minute reprieve to keep the child. As for running away, she pictured herself collapsing in a field from exhaustion and the baby dying in her arms. She couldn't let that happen to him.

'Put on this new blue suit I bought him,' said Lily in a cheerful mood for once, 'and make sure his nappy's not soiled. We want him to look as perfect as possible.' She added, 'Leave your suitcase in the hall before you go. It'll save you going back to your room to collect it, for there's no point in hanging around.'

Peggy thought that was very true.

The couple arrived on time but had to wait ten minutes before Peggy came into the hall carrying the child.

'What kept you?' said Lily, trying to keep her voice low as the woman smiled nervously at Peggy.

'He was crying and I had to get him quietened down,' said Peggy, handing over the baby wrapped tightly in a shawl.

'Well, he's quiet enough now,' said Lily with a brief glance at the child and a fawning smile at the woman who gazed at him in wonder and said, 'Isn't he beautiful?'

'He is,' said Lily, glaring at Peggy who stared dully ahead. The husband came forward to gaze over his wife's shoulder.

'He's certainly a fine boy,' he mumbled, as though slightly embarrassed by the whole affair.

The next moment they were leaving with Lily waving them goodbye. When the taxi had gone Peggy hurried to the door, relieved that Lily had walked past her without speaking. She couldn't have stood it if she had. The dog followed her and would possibly have come down the path and out the gate with her if she hadn't told it to go back. And only now that she was safely on the tram did she allow herself the luxury of wondering how long it would take the couple to discover the baby was dead.

POSTSCRIPT

Peggy had finished the last chapter of her novel, but wasn't entirely satisfied with it. She wondered if the ending was too abrupt, if perhaps there weren't enough details. She couldn't remember much of what had happened, only the judge saying that she'd murdered an innocent child and therefore was capable of murdering again. She was a danger to society and should be put away for the rest of her natural life. She'd been surprised at that. She hadn't thought she was capable of murdering again – she'd only killed her child to stop someone else having him. But apart from all this there was no one whose advice or opinion she could ask now that the duchess had gone. The duchess had not been good on advice but she'd always been strong on opinion.

'I'm going to donate my manuscript to the hospital,' she informed a patient in the day room who'd been watching television all morning with a baffled look on her face.

'Donate what?'

'My life story.'

'Oh I see. Are they going to make a film of it?'

'I don't think so. They haven't read it yet and I'm leaving today.'

'You're quite right,' said the patient. 'I'd leave too if I got half a chance.'

'The snag is I'll have to share a flat with someone.'

'That'll be nice,' said the patient, looking back at the television as if she'd said too much.

Peggy walked on to the veranda and remembered the duchess. She could imagine her sitting in her usual chair.

'They're letting me out,' she said, as if the duchess could hear her. 'After thirty odd years of being shunted from place to place for what I did they say I'm no longer a danger to society. Well, let's hope they're right.'

Then she went over and stared down through the railings. The bus shelter was empty. Just as well, she thought. She wasn't missing anything. Back in the ward she was handed the battered cardboard suitcase she'd come in with.

'I take it you're all packed and ready,' said the ward sister in a jolly tone.

Peggy said, looking confused, 'What do you mean, packed and ready? I'd hardly anything to pack.'

'It's a figure of speech,' said the sister. 'Don't pretend you're not glad to be leaving us. I'm sure you must be jumping with joy.'

'So I am,' said Peggy flatly, 'but I've been thinking, maybe I should take my manuscript. There's bound to be bits I should change and if I leave it behind I might forget what they are.' She broke off, adding anxiously, 'I can always send you a copy later.'

'Oh yes, your manuscript,' said the sister, barely suppressing a smile. 'I wouldn't worry about it if I was you. It will be fine the way it is and we're all dying to read it. Hurry now, the taxi's waiting.'

Before Peggy could say another word a young man took hold of her arm and led her out the back door of the hospital, explaining he was her social worker and would make sure she was all right. She scarcely listened. It had dawned on her she'd never see her manuscript again. They would have chucked it in the bin; that's why the ward sister had smiled. But she couldn't take it for granted.

'I'll have to go back,' she said and the young man's grip became tighter.

'I told you you'll be all right,' he said, pushing her into the back seat of the taxi then moving into the front beside the driver. The next thing they were off at what she considered an outrageous speed. She sank back and closed her eyes to stop feeling sick. When she opened them the taxi had stopped.

'Here we are,' said the young man. 'You can get out now. You're home.'

Laboriously she got out and stared up at a building whose height made her dizzy. She said, 'It doesn't look like home to me.'

'You'll love it once you're settled in. It's only a matter of getting used to it.'

He took the cardboard suitcase from the boot of the car. Peggy felt like telling him to throw it away but was too ashamed. Instead she asked him how far up the flat was and he told her the fourteenth floor, but not to worry, the lift was easy to manage and near her front door. Peggy stumbled towards it, her head spinning. The young man came at her side and pressed a button to open the doors. Inside the lift she told him not to come up with her, she would manage if he showed her where to press.

'Are you sure?' he said. 'I don't want you to get stuck halfway.'

'Don't worry, I'm not daft,' she said.

They both smiled at that then he handed her a key.

'Once you get out you'll see the number facing you, forty-four. You can't go wrong.'

After he'd gone she suddenly pressed the button, deciding that on the fourteenth floor she would throw herself from the first window she came to.

There would be no more anxiety or pain. She'd reached the end of her tether.

But when the lift stopped and the door opened she saw another one facing it. A white-haired old lady with the gaze of a child stood there saying, 'I'm Dorothy,' and holding out her hand. 'Are you my new flat-mate?' she asked. 'The other one disappeared. I think she was run over.'

Peggy, speechless, could only nod, return the handshake then follow the woman into the flat. The comfortable look of it pleasantly surprised her despite the slightly soiled sofa where a cat reclined on a cushion. A wilting bunch of flowers hung over a vase on the table.

'I hope you don't mind cats,' said the woman shyly. 'This one was a poor soul that didn't have a home.'

'Hmm,' said Peggy, sniffing the air. 'Judging by the smell in here we'd better get it a litter box or it'll be homeless once again.'

'Oh yes,' said Dorothy, clapping her hands like a child that's been promised a treat. 'I knew there was something I'd forgotten to get.'

'I suppose there will be other things as well,' said Peggy, punching a cushion from which the dust flew.

'There will be!' said the woman almost ecstatically. 'I'm always forgetting things and once I get up here I can't be bothered going out again. But now I'll make us a cup of tea. I expect you're dying for one.'

She dashed away leaving Peggy to stare round the room thinking that she was going to have her work cut out getting this place in order, but somehow she didn't mind. It was obvious the woman needed someone to look after her, as well as the cat. For a start it would learn to sleep on the floor. If this was to be her home, she certainly wasn't having a sofa covered in hairs.

A NOTE ON THE AUTHOR

Agnes Owens is the author of *Gentlemen of the West,*
Lean Tales (With James Kelman and Alasdair Gray),
Like Birds in the Wilderness, A Working Mother, and
People Like That. She lives in Scotland.